Toby Jones

—— AND THE ——
MYSTERY OF THE
TIME-TRAVEL TOUR

IT'S NOT JUST A GAME — IT'S TIME TRAVEL!

MICHAEL PANCKRIDGE

WITH BRETT LEE

Toby Jones

—— AND THE ——
MYSTERY OF THE TIME-TRAVEL TOUR

IT'S NOT JUST A GAME — IT'S TIME TRAVEL!

Angus&Robertson
An imprint of HarperCollins*Publishers*

All references to *Wisden Cricketers' Almanack* are by kind permission of
John Wisden & Co. Ltd.

Angus&Robertson
An imprint of HarperCollins*Publishers*, Australia

First published in Australia in 2005
by HarperCollins*Publishers* Pty Limited
ABN 36 009 913 517
A member of the HarperCollins*Publishers* (Australia) Pty Limited Group
www.harpercollins.com.au

HarperCollins*Publishers*
25 Ryde Road, Pymble, Sydney NSW 2073, Australia
31 View Road, Glenfield, Auckland 10, New Zealand
77–85 Fulham Palace Road, London W6 8JB, United Kingdom
2 Bloor Street East, 20th floor, Toronto, Ontario M4W 1A8, Canada
10 East 53rd Street, New York, NY 10022, USA

National Library of Australia Cataloguing-in-Publication data:

Panckridge, Michael, 1962– .
   Toby Jones and the mystery of the time-travel tour.
   For children aged ten to fourteen.
   ISBN 0 207 19998 1.
   1. Cricket – Juvenile fiction. I. Lee, Brett. II. Title.
A823.4

Cover photography by Alex Jennings; cricket memorabilia by Sport Memorabilia,
Sydney Antique Centre
Cover design by Christabella Designs based on original by Gayna Murphy
Illustrations on pages vi–vii by Steven Bray
Illustration on page 128 by Matt Stanton, HarperCollins Design Studio
Typeset in 10/15pt Stone Serif by Helen Beard, ECJ Australia Pty Ltd
Printed and bound in Australia by Griffin Press on 60gsm Bulky White

5 4 3 2 1   05 06 07 08

To the fielder at mid-on

who won't get a bowl and

bats down the order,

but who loves the game

as much as anyone

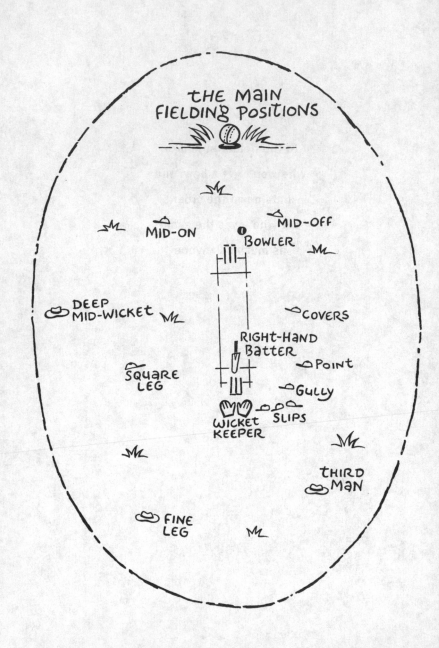

CLOSE UP OF THE CENTRE WICKET

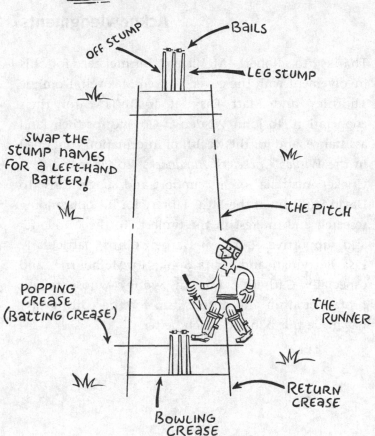

OFF STUMP

BAILS

LEG STUMP

SWAP THE STUMP NAMES FOR A LEFT-HAND BATTER!

THE PITCH

POPPING CREASE (BATTING CREASE)

THE RUNNER

RETURN CREASE

BOWLING CREASE

Acknowledgments

Thanks to Robert McVicker Burmeister for his involvement with the cover. To Neil Maxwell, Dominic Thornley and Matt Easy at Insite/ITM for their cooperation. To John Wisden & Co. Ltd for their kind assistance, and for the wealth of information contained in the *Wisden Cricketers' Almanack*s. To Peter Young at Cricket Australia for his support and suggestions. To David Studham at the MCC Library for his outstanding research and interest in the project. To the wonderful and supportive editors at HarperCollins, particularly Lisa Berryman and Liana Spoke in Melbourne, and especially Catherine Day in Sydney whose talent, professionalism and enthusiasm for the editing task has made this book so much better.

Contents

Foreword — xi

Glossary — xiii

Prologue 1

Chapter 1 — Runs on the Board 3

Chapter 2 — Virtual Cricket 12

Chapter 3 — Come back, Jim 22

Chapter 4 — Can It Get Any Hotter? 31

Chapter 5 — All Tied Up 42

Chapter 6 — Georgie Snaps 51

Chapter 7 — Toby Jones Opens on Boxing Day 57

Chapter 8 — The Double-wicket Comp 70

Chapter 9 — The Crazy Ride 78

Chapter 10 — Ben, the Good-looking Geek 88

Chapter 11 — The Surprise 98

Chapter 12 — Who's Pixie? 108

Chapter 13 — I'm Not the Paperboy 116

Chapter 14 — Timeless Travel Tours 126

Chapter 15 — Collapse 133

Chapter 16 — Out of the Blue 142

Chapter 17 — Ally or Jessica? 153

Chapter 18 — Back to Brisbane 163

Chapter 19 — So Close 175

Chapter 20 — Trouble for Ally 184

Brett Lee's Cricket Tips — 197
1960 Australia v West Indies Scorecard — 202
1930 England v Australia Scorecard — 205
Under-13 Southwestern Division
   Competition Rules and Draw — 208
   Scores and Ladders — 211
   The Finals Series — 213
Riverwall Scores and Statistics — 216
How to Play Double-wicket Cricket — 218
   Results of Riverwall's Double-wicket Competition — 220

Foreword

JUST like Toby Jones, I was obsessed by the game of cricket when I was a kid. I was always looking for ways to improve my game. I learned so much from my older brother Shane, and from seeking the advice of coaches. I read every cricket book I could get my hands on and I watched and learned from my idol: Dennis Lillee. Dennis was my inspiration, someone who I looked up to. I wanted to be just like him. (As it turned out, he has had a lot to do with my cricket career.)

I am sure you will find that this book is not only an excellent read, but also a very useful guide to the game of cricket. It contains lots of great hints and information that I hope you will be able to use to improve your own game.

When I first became involved in cricket, I had no idea where the game would take me. The opportunities and possibilities it has created for me are endless. Cricket has taught me many valuable lessons. Most of all it has shown me that if I always play hard and *enjoy* the opportunity of representing my country, I will be successful.

Every time I get asked to offer cricket advice to kids, my answer is always the same: enjoyment is the most important part of the game. When I am on the field, you will nearly always find me with a huge smile on my face. After suffering several injuries in my younger years, I have learned to make the most of every moment I get to play cricket.

This book reminds me of my own childhood days spent in the backyard with my brothers, always battling hard on the pitch to see who would be the champion player at the end of the day.

The *Toby Jones* series brings back truly great memories for me. I hope you enjoy reading the exciting new story *Toby Jones and the Mystery of the Time-Travel Tour*.

Brett Lee

Glossary

bails Two small pieces of wood that sit on top of the stumps. At least one has to fall off the stumps for a bowled or run-out decision to be made.

centre-wicket practice Team practice played out on a cricket field, as opposed to in the nets. Sometimes two or more bowlers are used, one after the other, to speed up the practice. If the batter goes out, he or she usually stays on for more batting practice.

covers A fielding position on the side of the wicket that the batter is facing, halfway between the bowler and the wicket keeper.

crease There are quite a few creases in cricket. They are lines drawn near the stumps that help the batters and bowlers know where they are in relation to the stumps.

fine leg A fielding position down near the boundary line behind the wicket keeper. Often a fast bowler fields in this position.

gully A close-in fielding position along from the slips — the fielders next to the wicket keeper.

lbw Stands for 'leg before wicket'. This is a way for a batter to be dismissed. If the bowler hits the pads of the batter with the ball, and he or she thinks that the ball would have gone on and hit the stumps, then the bowler can appeal for lbw. If the umpire is sure that the batter didn't hit the ball with the bat, then the batter may be given out.

leg-stump There are three stumps. This is the stump that is nearest the legs of the batter.

maiden If a bowler bowls an over and no runs are scored from it, then it is called a maiden.

mid-off A fielding position next to the bowler. It is on the off or bat side of the pitch as the batter looks down the wicket.

mid-on A fielding position next to the bowler. It is on the on or leg side of the pitch as the batter looks down the wicket.

no ball If a bowler puts his or her foot entirely over the return crease (the marked line) then it is a no ball and the batter can't be given out — unless it is a run-out.

off-stump The stump that is on the batting side of the batter.

third man A fielding position down behind the wicket keeper but on the other side of the fine leg fielder. The third man fielder is behind the slips fielders.

yorker The name for a delivery, usually bowled by a medium or fast bowler, that is pitched right up near the batter's feet. It is full pitched and fast.

Prologue

What wonders abound, dear boy, don't fear
These shimmering pages, never clear.
Choose your year, the Wisden name,
Find the page, your destined game,
Then find yourself a quiet place
Where shadows lurk, to hide your trace.

Whisper clear date, place or score
While staring, smitten; then before
(You hope) the close of play,
Be careful now, you've found the way.
So hide your home, your age, your soul
To roam this place and seek your goal.

Be aware that time moves on —
Your time, this time; none short, or long.
So say aloud two lines from here
Just loud enough for you to hear.
From a quiet spot, alone, unknown,
Back through time, now come — alone.

And never speak and never boast,
And never taunt, nor ever toast
This knowledge from your time you bring.
To woo the rest, their praises sing:
They wonder, and your star shines bright . . .
Just this once, this one short night?

But every word that boasts ahead
Means lives unhinged, broken, dead.
Don't meddle, talk, nor interfere
With the lives of those you venture near.
Respect this gift. Stay calm, stay clever,
And let the years live on forever.

1 Runs on the Board

'READ the poem to me again, Toby,' said Ally.

'Again?'

'Yeah. Slower.'

Pushing my bedroom door gently closed, I settled into the desk chair, adjusted the phone and started reading.

'Wow,' she sighed when I was finished. 'So, this all began on that excursion? Why didn't I pick the MCG?'

'Dunno. But that's where I met this amazing old guy in the library called Jim. He also has the gift — the ability to travel back to cricket matches in the past using *Wisden*s. They're those yellow cricket books I brought into school for my sports project, remember?'

'I remember.'

'Yeah, well, a few of us — Georgie, Rahul, Jay, Jimbo ... even Scott Craven — have actually travelled

3

back in time. And I thought it was about time you knew — especially since you're one of us now, playing cricket and everything. Jim was sent a diary and Jay found an old scorecard inside it. Anyone can travel with the scorecard; it's awesome. But Scott's uncle Phillip Smale has it now, and I know he'll use it. Sooner rather than later too.'

'He'll use it to travel back in time to a cricket match?' Ally asked. 'But isn't that just what you do, except you use a *Wisden*?'

I sighed. 'I do it to watch the cricket. Well, mainly,' I added, thinking of the scary times I'd had. 'Phillip Smale will do it to make money. To become famous.'

'Can he time travel without the scorecard?' Ally asked.

'Nope.'

'So, let's get the scorecard *from* him,' she said, like it was the easiest thing in the world.

'Well, it's not quite as simple as that,' I explained. 'Anyway, there's someone else I want to get back first.'

'What do you mean?'

'Jim is in Leeds, at the 1930 Test match he's dreamed of going to all his life. I took him there, and I left him. I'm really worried about him, Ally, he's like a grandpa to me.' Neither of us spoke for a moment. 'Anyway, I hope that fills you in.'

'Toby?'

'Yeah?'

'Thanks,' Ally said quietly. 'I'm really glad you told me.'

I smiled. 'No worries, Ally.'

Friday — afternoon

'Okay. We're batting first,' Mr Pasquali announced to the team. It was the semi-final against Benchley Park, the team we'd struggled against a few weeks ago. I was going to have to wait another day before I'd be steaming in to bowl that perfect off-cutter — the one I'd been dreaming about last night. 'Jono and I have discussed the batting order,' Mr Pasquali continued, nodding to our skipper.

'Yep,' Jono said, picking up the cue from our teacher and coach. 'Cameron and I are opening. Then Rahul, Jimbo, Toby and Ivo. Seventh is Ally, then Jay, Georgie, Gavin and Jason. Any volunteers for scoring?'

I wanted to watch the cricket without the hassle of keeping track of runs. Minh, our twelfth man, finally put up his hand.

Both our openers were warming up with some parents. I put my pads on carefully, then walked around the oval to sit behind the bowler. It was good playing at school, on our home ground. Mr Pasquali had been plugging the game all week: there was a note in the school newsletter and he'd even mentioned it at assembly on Friday. Quite a few kids had turned up to watch.

'If you make it through to the final we'll parade the entire team in front of the school assembly next week,' he'd told us.

'But not Scott Craven,' Ivo burst out.

'He's been a part of this team,' Mr Pasquali replied. 'Perhaps I'll give him the choice.' Scott had been our number-one strike bowler before he switched teams. Given the way his new team, the Scorpions, had played during the season, there was every chance they'd make it through to the grand final. Now that Scott had joined them that seemed even more likely.

We made a solid start with our batting. There was good, sound defence from our openers against the accurate deliveries but also some attacking shots on the looser ones. When Jono mistimed a pull shot and holed out to mid-wicket, we had already scored 43 runs at more than 5 an over.

Rahul played fantastically, fluently driving balls to the boundary. The Benchley Park umpire moved his fielders all over the place, but Rahul kept on finding the gaps.

When drinks were taken out, we were 1/81 and looking good. Both Rahul, and soon after, Cameron retired when they got their 40, and each got a huge clap as he came off the field.

With the score at 1/121, I strode out to the wicket to join Jimbo. There were still plenty of overs left, but I sensed that now was the time to crank up the scoring, especially with wickets up our sleeve. Jimbo agreed. He was already on eight (from two fours) when I joined him, and he hit another three boundaries before scoring his first single.

Each of his fours was greeted with beeping car horns and cheering from the boundary. Dad honked when I nudged my first two runs through point. For the next four overs we belted 37 runs off the tired Benchley attack.

'Looks like they're bringing on their openers again,' I said to Jimbo at the end of that fourth over, recognising the tall blond kid walking back to his mark.

'Good,' Jimbo said. 'Let's try and keep the tempo up.'

He hit two fours and a single from the next over and then had to retire. I found the fast bowlers harder to put away than the medium pacers and spinners. Martian belted a quick 11, but then Ally, Jay and Georgie went in fairly quick succession.

I was still in when Gavin marched out.

'Get out or retire,' he said to me. 'There are some big hitters waiting to come back and we haven't got much time.'

I was caught at deep mid-wicket that over, but Gavin only poked at the ball with Jason. I think Benchley Park preferred to keep them in; their fielders dropped two catches and their bowlers often bowled wide of the stumps. Finally, Gavin was caught off the last ball of the second last over.

'Your call, Jono,' I said. Rahul, Cameron and Jimbo were all padded up, ready to go.

'Jimbo, get out there and smash them,' Jono said.

And he did. After Jason scrambled a single to put Jimbo on strike, Jimbo blasted a two, three fours and a six off the last five deliveries.

Mr Pasquali was pleased, but reminded us that only half a game had been played. We'd scored 7/231. Batting was our strength, definitely. But tomorrow was going to be a lot harder, as we were without our strike bowler.

'Toby will be carrying a big load,' said Mr Pasquali, 'as will our other bowlers. We'll need outstanding support for them in the field. That's our focus for Saturday. Now off you go and have a relaxing evening — you've all earned it. Well done!'

Georgie elbowed me. 'Oh, my God,' she said. 'Look!'

Walking straight towards us across the oval were Scott and his uncle, Phillip Smale. No one said anything as they approached, until Mr Pasquali noticed them.

'Scott! How was your game,' he asked. Scott was playing in the other semi-final at the Scorpions' home ground, against Motherwell State School.

He shrugged. 'Got a few,' he said, looking down.

'A few! He took 7 for 17 off eight overs, with three maidens. It's got to be a record: I'll be checking the files this evening. In *my* office,' Smale boasted, looking at Georgie and me.

I won't ever forget the ordeal Georgie and I went

through in Smale's office at the Scorpions' clubrooms last weekend.

'Well done, Scott. Terrific,' said Mr Pasquali. He sounded genuinely pleased.

'We'll be pressing for the outright win, of course,' Phillip Smale persisted. 'We've already won the game. Got them all out for —'

'Uncle Phillip, leave it, okay?' Scott muttered.

The rest of the team went about packing up. No one was taking much interest in Scott, though there were a few curious glances at his uncle.

Smale turned towards Dad. 'Peter, how are you?'

'Oh, hello, Phillip.'

'I just wanted to mention that we're looking at making some changes over at the library at the MCG. Actually, I thought I'd be pulling out of there, you know. That was my intention, but they really do need me.'

I caught Scott's eye, before he looked down again.

'Yes, unfortunately we're doing some upgrades, so there'll be no visitors for some time.' Mr Smale looked at me. 'But I'm sure Toby here will find other things to do.'

'Well, I'm sure he will, Phillip. We've got the *Wisden* Studio to work on, haven't we, son?'

'The *Wisden* Studio?'

'It'll be a step back in time, won't it, Toby? We're looking to get as many copies of *Wisden*s as we can. And Jim Oldfield is going to open it.'

Smale's jaw dropped. 'B ... but, well, th ... that's —'

'C'mon, Dad,' I grumbled, dragging him away. 'You don't want to listen to him.'

'Bye, Phillip!' Dad called over his shoulder. There was no reply.

'Nice one, Dad,' I murmured under my breath in the car on the way home.

'What's that?'

'Want some help in the studio after tea?'

'Sure,' Dad replied, looking pleased.

But I didn't end up helping out because Georgie phoned me after dinner.

'Toby, there's supposed to be a poster up on Smale's office window about a virtual cricket machine. Ally and I are going to check it out. Are you coming?'

'What, to the Scorpions' clubrooms?' I said doubtfully, thinking of the swarms of Scorpion kids and parents who would be celebrating their semi-final thrashing of Motherwell that afternoon. 'Georgie, I don't know — Scott and Smale and everyone else'll be there.'

'So? We'll just look in the window, then leave. What's the big deal?'

'Nothing, except that Smale mentioned his office in a funny way after the game this arvo. I didn't like the way he said "In *my* office".'

'Tobler, you're getting paranoid. C'mon.' Georgie was beginning to sound frustrated.

'Since when have you called me Tobler?'

'Since you've started taking girls home from cricket practice,' she sniggered.

'What do you —' But I was talking to a long, high-pitched beeping noise. I could imagine Georgie chuckling as she put down the phone.

'Just going for a quick ride!' I announced, to no one in particular.

'Can I come?' Natalie, my younger sister called.

'No,' I yelled back, banging the front door shut. I opened it again, feeling a bit guilty. 'Next time, Nat. I'm just going up to Georgie's.'

'Then why don't you walk?' she shouted from the living room.

'Because!' I shouted back, lamely.

The last Australian to take all 10 wickets in an innings was Ian Brayshaw in 1967. He was playing for Western Australia against Victoria, in Perth. His figures were 17.6 overs (there were eight balls per over), 4 maidens and 10 wickets for 44 runs.

2 Virtual Cricket

Friday — evening

'WHAT'S the camera for?' I said, exasperated. Georgie was forever bringing along extra things: a camera, clothing, keys, binoculars ... Mind you, they'd mostly come in handy before, but I didn't think the Scorpions would want someone taking photos around their club.

'Relax, Tobler,' she said, packing the camera into its case.

'My name's not Tobler.'

'Yeah? You don't say that to Ally.'

'I never get a chance —'

'Hi, Tobler,' Ally called, as she stepped out of Georgie's house. 'I'm glad you could come.'

'Oh hi, Ally,' I said, wondering if she'd heard me.

'See?' Georgie hissed.

'Well, let's go and check this poster thing out,' I said, hastily changing the subject. I wish I could just talk cricket, 24/7. Life'd be so much easier.

Sure enough, there were plenty of kids and adults gathered around the Scorpions' clubrooms enjoying a barbecue as we rode up. A few of the kids were playing cricket with some of the dads, but most of the crowd were sitting around in plastic chairs, drinking beer or cola. A new scoreboard, displaying the afternoon's scores, stood prominently by the main door to the clubrooms.

'Motherwell all out for 53. Scorpions 2 for 89 in reply,' I remarked, quietly.

'Well let's hope the scoreboard looks totally different next week,' said Ally.

We rode up to the building, where a large and colourful poster took up half of one of Smale's office windows. Georgie pulled out her camera and took a quick photo, but we'd hardly had time to look when Scott Craven himself marched out of the clubrooms and over to us.

'So, what brings you all here?' he sneered, before taking a swig from the can he was holding.

'We just missed you, Scott, that's all,' Georgie said, airily.

'Yeah, well, beat it. I told you, Jones, that it's all over. Maybe you didn't get the message clear? Maybe you want me to give it to you a different way?'

Scott had been involved the last time we'd travelled back to 1930, and he was spooked by the whole thing.

'Gee, Scott, thanks for the thought.'

'C'mon, let's go,' Georgie said, as Scott seemed about to reply.

We spun around and sped off.

'Hey, I never even got to read the poster,' Ally cried once we were several streets away from the Scorpions ground.

'Nor me,' I added.

'That's why I brought this, sillies,' Georgie laughed, holding the little digital camera up in the air. 'Toby, can we do this at your house? Mum'll be on the computer at home.'

We downloaded the photo of the poster onto the computer in the living room. It looked awesome. There was a big TV screen, a cricket pitch with real stumps and a complicated box of gadgets and dials, switches and buttons. There was also a picture of a headset.

'Survive the Master Blaster at Lyndale Shopping Centre!' I read.

'So how does it work?' Georgie asked, looking at the fine print.

'State-of-the-art futuristic technology puts you into a virtual game of cricket. Go up against the might of the greatest bowlers in the world,' Ally read.

'Cool,' Georgie and I sighed at the same time.

'Face the world's fastest deliveries coming at you at over 150 kilometres per hour. Completely safe, Master Blaster is set to sweep the world in the next few years. But trials are continuing, and luckily for you they are about to happen in *your* home town.'

'That'd be like facing Brett Lee. How is that safe?' Georgie asked.

'It's virtual — that's the thing. You don't get hit, you don't get hurt. It's all pretend.'

'No way.' Georgie sounded very impressed. 'This sounds so cool. When is it?'

'Next Friday. Hey, why hasn't Mr Pasquali told us about this? Why doesn't anyone know?' Ally said.

'Scott knows. Mr Smale knows. Probably all the Scorpions know,' I said, looking out of the window. 'Gosh! Imagine facing up to Brett Lee.'

'You can have him. I'll wait for someone a bit slower, thanks.'

'Maybe Michael Clarke? I thought you said you fancied him,' Ally said, teasing Georgie. 'You like the blonds, don't you?' Georgie gave her a shove, and suddenly they were cavorting about on the floor. I read, then reread the poster, until someone grabbed my leg and hauled me over onto the carpet.

'Spoilsport,' Ally cried, as I bounced back to the chair in front of the computer.

I logged onto the Net to see if I could get any more info about this Master Blaster thing; I was hooked. I looked up Master Blaster, virtual cricket, even Lyndale Shopping Centre, but nothing of interest came up. For a few minutes I fiddled around with some dodgy-looking cricket games with cruddy graphics and basic layouts. They weren't at all what I was imagining virtual cricket would be like.

15

'Ally,' Mum called from somewhere. 'Can you give your mum a ring?'

'So, Toby, Jim is stuck in England —' Ally said.

'He's not stuck,' Georgie protested. 'He's just there.'

'He *is* stuck,' I muttered.

'Toby, that's where he wants to be. He said so himself.'

'How is he stuck exactly?' Ally asked, looking curious.

'Haven't you got a phone call to make?' Georgie asked.

'It can wait five minutes.'

I looked at Ally. 'Jim is in England because —'

'Toby! You might as well write something in the school newsletter,' Georgie interrupted, throwing up her hands.

'Sorry, am I out of line here or something?' Ally asked.

Georgie sighed. 'Sorry, of course you're not. It's just that I reckon the more people that know, the more dangerous this is for Toby and anyone else who knows.'

'Well, go on,' Ally said, looking at me, not sounding at all concerned about anyone's safety.

'Jim never got to see the famous Leeds Test match from 1930, the one where Don Bradman made over 300 runs in a day. Jim was a kid, living over there, but he was too sick to go to the game. So I took him —'

'But, Jim's a time traveller too, isn't he? He has the same gift as you?'

'Yes. And I know what you're going to say: why didn't he go back on his own?'

'Exactly,' Ally said.

'He was warned never to return to that particular time alone. It was like, really serious. And he never did.'

'So, Toby took him there,' Georgie said, like she wanted to close the matter.

'And left him there,' I added. No one spoke. Ally pressed her lips together. She was stewing over something.

'Well, why don't you go back and check if he's okay?' she asked, finally.

'Ally, that's the dumbest idea in the world. Don't you get it? Toby *can't* go back. Nor can I. We've already been back twice ... three times ... how many times, Toby?'

'Um —'

'Exactly. It's impossible. If you see yourself or get close to yourself, which is what could happen if we went back, then there's supposed to be this powerful force that smashes your two bodies together.'

'And then?' Ally asked.

Georgie looked over at me. I shrugged.

'I think it's bad,' I said, quietly.

'*I* could check on Jim,' Ally said, almost in a whisper.

'Ally, you haven't got this gift,' Georgie moaned, closing her eyes.

'How do you know?' Ally asked.

'I could take you there,' I said, slowly.

'Toby, you know you shouldn't,' Georgie scolded.

'You know what some of the last words Jim said to me were?' I asked her.

Georgie shrugged.

'He said that Dad and I were like family to him. And families stick together, right?'

'Right,' Ally said, eagerly.

'Families look out for each other, yeah?' I looked over at Georgie.

She nodded. 'I guess.'

'So, I've got to go back.'

'Then I'm coming too,' Georgie said, jumping to her feet. 'We just need to arrive at the end of the day.'

'You been thinking about that?' I asked her, grinning.

Georgie looked at me sheepishly.

'Yeah, well, it crossed my mind,' she chuckled.

Ally went to make her phone call while Georgie and I hurried upstairs to my bedroom to find the 1931 *Wisden*. I reached up and pulled it down from my shelves. It was by far the oldest and rarest in my growing collection. The cover was a faded yellow, old, softish and a bit leathery.

We came out of the room to find Ally at the foot of the stairs, a smirk on her face.

'You often go into Tobler's bedroom, Georgie?'

'Since I was about three years old,' Georgie fired back, quick as a flash. Georgie and I had been neighbours and best mates for about 10 years now; she lived only a few doors down. I don't think it had occurred to either of us before that there was anything weird about her being there. But maybe, from Ally's point of view, it seemed a bit odd.

'Come on up,' I called to her.

'Everything okay?' Georgie asked Ally as she entered the room.

'Yep. Mum's coming round to pick me up in an hour,' she said, looking around. I felt a bit self-conscious with her gazing about at my things like that.

'C'mon, Ally, over here,' I said, sitting down on the floor. 'Georgie, the Leeds Test is on page 33. You've got to find a bit where it talks about the end of the day. Just read —'

'What about our clothes, Toby?' Georgie asked, stretching out her light blue singlet.

'Do you remember ever seeing three kids in blue, red and off-white tops running about the place at Leeds?' I asked her.

'Nope,' she said, with a sly smile.

'Nor me. That means we made it without being noticed. C'mon, start reading. There's usually a bit of an intro and then it gets into the summary.'

I watched Georgie scan down the page, mumbling to herself. Georgie saw words, just as she should. But when *I* looked at *Wisden*s the words and numbers were lost in a swirling confusion that dipped and spun in a slow, twisting spiral. With effort, I could focus on a date, place or score, and then the fun would begin.

'Can I try?' Ally asked, reaching out for the book. Georgie passed it to her.

'Well?' we asked simultaneously.

'Looks pretty boring to me,' she said.

'Can you read it?' I asked.

'Which bit?'

'Here, give it to me. I'll do it.' Georgie snatched the *Wisden* back. Ally shrugged, put her chin on her hands and waited. I guessed she hadn't really taken in what was about to happen. I turned back to Georgie, who held her finger to a spot well down the page.

'Here you go,' she said.

'You sure this is the right spot?' I asked. 'What does it say?'

'Yes,' she said. 'Bradman's already made 105 runs. You can't do that before lunch on the first day of a Test match, can you?' she said.

'Don Bradman's different,' I replied. But I didn't recall seeing him with that many runs on my previous visits.

'Ally, this'll feel really weird, but trust me, it works. Grab Toby's hand.' As Georgie reached out for my other hand, I leaned in closer to see where her finger was pointing.

Almost straight away a capital 'B' emerged from the mess, then disappeared. I stared at the spot where it had vanished till it emerged again, this time with some more letters after it. I looked to the right for Bradman's score. A number appeared.

'How many runs?' I whispered, staring at the page.

'105,' Georgie replied.

'One ... hundred ... and ... Georgie, are you sure ...'

My voice trailed away, becoming separate from my body. I felt Ally's grip tighten, her fingernails digging into me. I squeezed back, a whooshing sensation surging over and all around me like a breaking wave. Just as quickly as it had come the rushing noise stopped and we were sitting in the sunshine on a patch of grass by an old wooden fence.

The best bowling figures ever recorded were produced by Englishman Hedley Verity. Playing for Yorkshire against Nottingham in 1932, he achieved the amazing result of 19.4 overs, 16 maidens, taking 10 wickets for only 10 runs.

3 Come back, Jim

'TOBY?' Ally breathed, still holding my hand. 'We're in Leeds?'

'Yes,' I said, looking round.

'Where is Leeds?' she asked tentatively.

'Leeds? In England, Ally. You are standing in England, over 75 years ago. What do you think?'

Not surprisingly, Ally stood there silently, amazed, staring at the crowd in front of her. I, on the other hand, was getting very familiar with the surroundings. The entrance to the ground was away to our right, the stand where Jim was sitting a little further around.

I nodded at the scoreboard. 'Look, Bradman's on 113 already. And Woodfull's still in. Georgie, maybe it still is the first session. Let's not do anything stupid,' I said, turning back to the girls. 'You stay right here, and I'll go and check on Jim. I want to give him one last chance. That's all.'

'That's *all*?' Georgie queried, tilting her head.

'Yes, I promise. I'll be back in three minutes, tops. Then we're out of here, okay?'

'I'm freaked,' Ally shivered. 'Three minutes is three too many if you ask me.'

'Ally, it's cool. I promise,' Georgie said, squeezing her arm, trying to reassure her. Ally looked pale.

'Won't be a moment.'

I raced off towards the stand as a burst of applause swept around the ground. Another Bradman boundary, I thought, noticing a fielder jogging out to retrieve the ball. I reached the steps of the stand, and suddenly felt a violent tug. It was as if someone had grabbed me round the waist and was hauling me backwards. The air was forced out of my lungs and I gasped for breath.

''Ere lad, c'mon.' A man was talking to me, but the pain was terrible and I couldn't answer. I fell back, crashing onto the first step. It seemed like a gigantic vacuum cleaner was pulling at me and sucking out my insides. I wrapped my arms tightly around myself as other arms reached down to move me. I was dying inside. Something was leaving me and I was scared witless. I tried to open my eyes and respond to the concerned voices but they became distant.

Then suddenly everything became quiet and calm. The fever that had gripped me eased and I drifted away. I seemed to be floating. Hundreds of images flashed across my mind, a speeding whir of snapshots from my life: Natalie crying; Mum driving; Dad standing in the back yard, hands on hips; the view from my bedroom window ...

'Toby?' The images slowed. I saw a yellow *Wisden*; Scott Craven's head slamming into a toilet door ...

'My dear boy, look at me.'

And Jim. The stooped, gentle figure with his lined face, smiling at me in the library at the MCG ...

'Please, Toby.' A hand was grasping my shoulder. Slowly I opened my eyes, the pain in my head awful. The pale, ghostly image of Jim's face hovered over me.

'Jim?' I felt my lips moving, but no sound came out. I licked them and tried again.

'Look at me, Toby,' Jim said, sternly. But his face disappeared, and with relief I again closed my eyes, sinking back into the wonderful sleep that was overtaking me.

'*Toby Jones!*' Something tickled my face, and I felt my eyes being prised open.

'Jim?' I gasped.

'Be strong, Toby. Open your eyes and look at me.' I knew he was shouting, yet his voice was barely a whisper. He seemed so far away.

'J ... Jim? W ... what's happening?' I couldn't move. Other faces started to appear and I could hear faint noises of life around me. Jim put a hand to my face and wiped away the tears. There was blood on his hand, which he cleaned with a handkerchief.

'What happened?' I asked again.

'You met yourself,' he grimaced, 'and I've brought you back.' He pursed his lips.

'*I saw myself?*'

'Perhaps for a moment there were *two* Toby Joneses present in the same time and space. And of course there is only room for one. But possibly not,' Jim replied, standing up. He held out a hand for me. The onlookers had drifted away, lured by the cricket. 'Come along. You obviously came back to fetch me, hmm?'

'Jim, I couldn't leave you here. What about the two hours? What would have happened to you after two hours?'

'Well, it would appear that this time travel is actually invigorating me, Toby. I think perhaps that I am immune to the dangers of staying too long. But, believe me, if I weren't, then quietly slipping away without burdening anyone wouldn't be too bad.' Jim saw my look of horror. 'Well, I saw Bradman play some beautiful strokes. Not the 300 runs in a day that I might have, but one takes what is offered. Isn't that right, Toby?'

'Will you come back with me, Jim?' I asked, struggling to my feet. I felt like I'd just gone 10 rounds with Scott Craven in a certain toilet block.

'Of course,' he said. 'Lead the way.'

Jim put an arm on my shoulder and we walked back to where Georgie and Ally were still standing, trying to blend into the background in their bright red and blue tops.

'Georgie girl, how good it is to see you again. It's only been half an hour since I saw you last, but how much time has gone by in your life?' Jim asked. Ally was looking totally bewildered.

'Not long, Jim. About a day,' she chuckled.

'Ah, good. These old bones are used to a bit of travel, so a day away won't be too much of a bother. Nothing new, then, for me to learn?'

'Well,' I said aloud, thinking of the virtual cricket machine, 'there may be one thing. But I'll tell you about it later. Come on, everyone. Hold on.' I felt better by the minute.

'But won't someone see us?' Ally asked, taking my hand again.

'That is an interesting question,' Jim chuckled. He didn't seem at all put out that I'd come back to rescue him.

'Jim, you don't mind coming back, then?'

'My dear boy, I've been waiting for you,' he said. 'Perhaps hoping you might arrive a little later, but alas. Now, let's be gone.'

> *Then find yourself a quiet place*
> *Where shadows lurk, to hide your trace.*

I recited the words aloud — and in a flash we had returned to my bedroom.

'So, no one saw us?' Ally asked, looking from me to Jim.

'Jim. Jim Oldfield,' he said to Ally, smiling. 'Delighted to meet you, my dear,' he added, holding his hand out to her.

'Oh, hi. I'm Ally.' She shook his hand.

'No one saw you, my dear,' said Jim. 'It's one of the peculiar things about *Wisden* travel, quite unexplained. Some sort of time warp takes place. Those in the area temporarily cannot see into the space occupied by the travellers. I'm afraid I don't know much —'

'Toby? Are you in there?' Natalie called from the hallway.

'Just coming, Nat. You wanna play corridor cricket? Ally here wants to play on your team.'

'Oh, cool. I love Ally,' she yelled. We heard her footsteps retreating down the hall.

'She's not the only one,' Georgie mumbled. At least, that's what I thought she mumbled. We all ignored her.

'Well, now,' said Jim. 'There's just the small task of removing myself from your home, Toby Jones. I think it would be most unwise for me to stroll down your stairway and greet your dear parents at this point, don't you?'

'Um, yes. I guess so,' I said.

'That wouldn't be good,' Georgie laughed. 'Ally and I will go and suss it out. Ally, get Nat to show you how to play corridor cricket. I'll wait at the bottom of the stairs and signal when the coast's clear, okay?'

'Good old practical Georgie,' Jim said, nodding approvingly. Ally just looked at each of us in turn, shaking her head in wonder.

'Don't worry, Ally,' I told her. 'You'll get used to it.'

'Oh, well, that's a relief. For a minute I thought I'd shifted to another planet.'

Georgie opened the door, and Jim took a few steps back to be out of view of the hallway, just in case.

'Ally, are you okay?' I asked her quietly.

She took a deep breath. 'Yep, I think so. Toby, I was totally freaked out. But you know what?' I had a feeling I knew what she was about to say. 'I want to go again.' I was right. 'Weird, huh?'

'Yep. Very strange.'

Ally nodded and headed out the door to follow Georgie downstairs.

'I met myself, didn't I, Jim?' I said.

'Yes, Toby, you did. Luckily for us travellers, it's an experience that we are more able to deal with than those we carry.'

'You mean like my friends?'

'Yes. They are far more vulnerable to the problems that can arise.' Jim had picked up a cricket ball from my desk and was gently fingering the seam.

I had grown really close to Jim in the time that I'd known him. There was something vulnerable about him that needed protecting. He was old, and no amount of wisdom could make up for the fact that he was fragile. But I needed him. The time travel was part of my life, and I wanted Jim to be a part of it as well.

'Jim, would you come and live with us?' I said. I had no idea where he lived. His life outside the library at the MCG was a complete mystery, and maybe he had nowhere to go. The only other place

I'd seen him was in a hospital. He never spoke of a family.

'One thing at a time, Toby,' Jim said, smiling at me.

'Hey,' Georgie called from down below.

I stuck my head round the door, and she gave me the thumbs up. 'Let's go, Jim.'

He picked up the 1931 *Wisden* lying on the floor and shuffled out. I raced ahead of him, bounding down the stairs. I'd just reached the bottom when the phone rang.

'Got it,' shouted Dad. A door banged shut.

I spun around, urging Jim to follow me. I took his arm and gently guided him towards the back door, then steered him away from the house and to the little side gate next to Dad's new studio.

'This is where the fire was,' I said quietly. 'It used to be a boring old garage. Now Dad's contemplating a permanent move.'

'Most impressive,' Jim said, eyeing the bookshelves behind the double-glass doors.

'Jim, can you make it to my game tomorrow? We're in the semi-final against Benchley Park, up at the school oval.' The words were just tumbling out of my mouth.

We'd made it to the laneway. 'How will you get home?' There was a pause. I looked into Jim's eyes. 'Where is home?'

The question hung between us. He smiled, then turned away.

'Jim?'

'You get a good night's sleep, Toby Jones,' he called without looking back. 'You've got a lot of bowling to do tomorrow.'

I watched him walk away, wondering where and when we would meet again.

I also wondered how he knew that I'd be bowling tomorrow. Maybe it was a 50/50 bet. But then Jim didn't seem the betting type.

I turned and jogged back inside for the promised game of corridor cricket.

The best bowling figures in a Test match are held by Jim Laker of England. Playing against Australia in Manchester in 1956, he took all 10 wickets in Australia's second innings (and nine in the first). He bowled 51.2 overs in that innings, with 23 maidens and 10 wickets for 53 runs.

4 Can It Get Any Hotter?

Saturday — morning

'IT'S a boiler,' Dad sighed, strolling into the kitchen the following morning. 'It's going to be an absolute belter. Toby, get Benchley Park out nice and quick, you hear me?'

'You bet, Dad.' I searching his face for any clues that he suspected anything was up after last night. But he padded about in his bare feet, boxer shorts and straggly hair, as on most other mornings, totally focused on getting his breakfast organised.

'Hey, Dad? There's a new virtual reality machine down at the shopping centre. Can we go and check it out sometime?'

'Virtual what?' he asked, attending to the toaster.

'Virtual reality. You know — real, but not real.'

'Real, but not real?' he repeated slowly.

'Well, yeah. Almost real. Virtually real. You know.'

'Hmm, not exactly, but I guess I'm going to find out soon enough, aren't I?' He winced as his finger touched the hot edge of the toaster.

'Thanks, Dad.' I looked at the clock. 'Ten minutes and we're out of here, okay?' I called, getting up.

'Ten minutes,' he said, licking his finger.

I couldn't believe the heat. The air was still, and it was hard to breathe. Even at 8.20 in the morning the temperature was 27 degrees, and Dad said it was expected to climb to 42 degrees. You could smell the dryness as well as a faint hint of smoke.

'Let's hope we don't have to worry about a bushfire,' Dad said, sniffing the air as we got out of the car. 'Total fire bans bring out the total idiots.' He looked at me. 'Sounds dumb, I know, but make sure you do a proper stretch.' Dad hauled out his deckchair and the enormous Saturday newspaper, and settled down in the shade of a large gum tree.

I grabbed my gear and walked over to Mr Pasquali's car to help him with the kit.

'It's a hotty, Mr P,' I said, pulling out the stumps.

'Short spells today, Toby. Hats and zinc too,' he added, looking up at the sky. 'Thanks for helping.'

More cars arrived and soon the team was in the outfield tossing a ball around. I went to measure my run-up, though I could easily see where I'd scuffed a mark in the grass lots of other times during the season.

I strolled in to the middle and rolled my arm over

a few times until Mr Pasquali called us together for the traditional pre-game pep talk.

'Now I don't need to tell you to be sensible out here today. I want you to wear hats, sunscreen, even sunglasses if you've got them,' he began. Already there were beads of sweat on his face. 'It'll be hard work for their batters too, but we must support our bowlers. Short spells, Jono,' he said, turning to our captain. Jono nodded.

'I'm not going to interfere with bowling changes or fielding positions,' Mr Pasquali continued, 'but I'll say this. Any suggestions should go through the captain, and I want there to be suggestions. I want you to be alert to what the batters are doing, alert to any weaknesses you see, alert to anything at all.' He paused, looking around at each of us in turn.

'I've coached a few Riverwall teams in my time, but none quite as good as this one. Let's show the parents, and the opposition, what sort of a team you are.'

Jono tossed me the new ball. How would our bowling line-up rate now that Scott Craven wasn't a part of it? Time would tell. I had to stand up and take over the responsibility for leading the attack. I'd been in Scott's shadow all season — now was my big chance to lead from the front.

My start couldn't have been worse. I should have pulled out of my run-up, but instead I stuttered up to the crease, my rhythm and strides all over the place. I overstepped the popping crease by a mile and bowled a wayward delivery that Ivo took in front of Jono at first slip.

I slowed down for the rest of the over and wasn't even thinking of taking wickets; I just wanted to put the ball in the right spot.

'Okay, you've got that one under your belt, Toby. You've got to attack now,' Jimbo said. He'd jogged all the way over from the covers to fire me up.

'It felt shocking,' I told him.

'Mate, it looked shocking. But that's because you weren't relaxed. Next over, just let it go and see what happens.' I nodded, feeling better for the advice.

Our top four bowlers — Cameron, Jono, Rahul and me — were in the top six of the batting line-up as well. We were a team that fell away quickly. Ivo was a really good keeper. He had won his spot back from Ally who had filled in for most of the season after Ivo's bad accident, when his bike collided with a car. Ally was an awesome softballer with great reflexes and a strong throwing arm, but she didn't appear very comfortable without the keeper's gloves on.

Georgie, Jay, Gavin (who was really grumpy now that his best mate, Scott Craven, had left the team) and Jason loved their cricket but were really just filling up the numbers.

I looked over at Jimbo as I took the ball for my next over. He gave me the thumbs up. I tried to clear all the negative thoughts from my mind. I'd run in to bowl a thousand times without ever thinking of my stride pattern, yet suddenly I was feeling like a total loser.

'C'mon Tobes,' Jimbo called from the covers, clapping his hands. A few others joined in. 'Time for some action.' The batter nonchalantly looked around the field, then settled down over his bat.

I took a deep breath, made one final check that the small plastic disc I use to mark my run-up was exactly where it should be, then steamed in. Somewhere, someone was clapping but I pressed on, striding out, my paces lengthening as I approached the pitch.

This time it felt perfect. The seam of the ball stayed upright and the ball cut back fractionally from the off side, thudding into the batsman's pads. It was probably 15 kilometres per hour faster than any ball from the previous over.

'Howzat!' I screamed, jumping in the air and turning to the umpire. I could tell straight away by his grim look that he was going to put up his finger. And he did.

'Yeah!' I roared, turning round and charging down to the slips.

'Bloody beauty!' Jono cried, clapping me on the shoulder. The rest of the team charged in.

'That's more like it, Toby Jones,' Jimbo said, his fists clenched.

The rest of the over played out uneventfully — the kid who went in for Benchley at first drop, a guy called Edison Rocker, was easily their best batter — but I felt much better. Every ball was on target.

It's amazing what a wicket can do for your confidence. Suddenly I was feeling on top of the world again, desperate to get another crack at the batsmen.

'Two more overs, Toby, maybe three if you snag another wicket,' Jono called as we changed ends. And then the day improved even more when I noticed Jim sitting in Dad's chair with Dad nowhere to be seen. He was probably off scrounging another chair. I gave Jim a wave and he waved back.

I didn't take another wicket in that spell. By the first drinks break Benchley Park had still only lost the one batsman and were looking settled, though they weren't scoring quickly.

'We've just got to dry them up,' Jono said, guzzling down some ice-cold cordial. 'It's really important that we keep the runs down. No wides, no misfields.'

'And we need to back up in the field,' Jimbo said. 'They're probably going to start looking for the quick singles to break things up a bit.'

It was great how Jimbo was getting more involved. This was only his third game for us. Years earlier his dad had banned him from playing cricket because he'd walked away from the game himself after being hit by a vicious ball. His anger had carried through to poor Jimbo, but luckily Mr Temple, Jimbo's dad, had had a change of heart. Luck for us, too. Jimbo was a brilliant batter and his knowledge of cricket was amazing.

And he was right about backing up too. During the second over after drinks, the batters sprinted through for a single. Jimbo charged in, scooped up the ball and took a shot at the stumps at the bowler's end, missing by inches. Cameron tried to gather in the ball, but it flew past him.

'Again!' Edison Rocker screamed, not realising that I had actually stopped Jimbo's throw from going to the boundary with an enormous dive to my left. I flicked the ball back to Cameron, who was still by the stumps at the bowler's end.

Edison's batting partner was run-out by about eight metres.

'I'm going to call you Prophet,' I laughed at Jimbo. He'd predicted exactly what had just happened.

But as the morning grew hotter, some of us started to drag our feet. Two catches went down, and several misfields and sloppy throws crept into our game.

Jono, Jimbo and I tried to keep everyone positive and motivated but it was an effort, particularly because Benchley Park didn't really look like a threat.

Edison Rocker got his 40, but there weren't any other quality batters in the team. And although Jay and Jason were belted for a couple of fours each, it was just a matter of time before Benchley collpased.

With ten overs left Jono tossed the ball to me.

I decided to put the heat out of my mind and concentrate on line and length. There was a chance for some wickets as the batsmen were starting to play loose shots to up the scoring rate.

My first two balls were off target, but the third was spot on. Aimed at off-stump, it caught the seam and deviated left, catching the bat's outside edge. Martian took a ripper catch low down in front of Jono.

I slowed up the next two deliveries and the new guy played them easily enough. Ambling in for the last ball of the over, I was hoping the batter was expecting the same again, but I swung my arm over quickly, pitching the ball on a shorter length.

At the last moment he hoicked his bat to keep the ball off his chest. The ball ballooned away to my left and I dived, catching it just centimetres from the ground.

The game died quickly after that. The Benchley Park coach made sure all his team got a brief hit, retiring a couple of the batters early. One kid was so annoyed that he swore then threw his bat about five metres into the air.

Benchley Park had fallen short of our total by just under 70 runs, but our celebrations were pretty subdued. Maybe it was the weather. Maybe it was the fact that we hadn't really won anything — yet. Scott Craven and the Scorpions were on most people's minds as we packed up the gear, folded away the chairs and headed off to our cars.

'Dad,' I said, 'can Jim come around to our place this arvo?' But as I spoke I saw a taxi turn into the ground and Jim wave an arm at it.

'I already asked, Tobes. But he said he'd come around tonight if he can.' Dad smiled, ruffling my hair. 'You're really very fond of him, aren't you?'

'He's shown me some very interesting things,' I said, watching Jim walk towards us.

'Well played, Toby. Your bowling is most impressive,' Jim said.

'Not my first over,' I mumbled.

'No, indeed. But that too was impressive. You were able to put it behind you and bowl from then on with good pace and rhythm.'

Jim said goodbye and walked slowly over to the taxi. Watching him, I remembered that he really was an old man.

'Toby?' Ally called, holding up a bottle. 'You want the last drink?' I didn't, but I headed over to her anyway. 'Um — er, Toby?' she asked quietly, looking up at me from beside the Esky. 'You reckon I can go on another cricket trip?'

'Well, I guess,' I said, cautiously. My experiences of taking friends to faraway places weren't all good. Rahul in India was the scariest: he'd paid me no attention at all, wanting to go off on his own. It was like he'd been possessed.

'You don't look so sure?' she said, eyeing me closely.

'Well, it's just that —'

'You think Georgie'd get a bit upset?' Her voice had risen slightly. I looked around but nearly everyone had gone or were in their cars about to leave.

'You see, I took Rahul to the Tied Test —'

'The Tied Test? Cool, that would have been exciting. Did you see the run-out?'

'Run-out?' I asked.

'There's that famous photo of the West Indian dude who did that amazing run-out,' Ally said.

We were talking about different games. She was thinking about the Test match between Australia and the West Indies in 1960, played in Brisbane. It was another of Dad's favourites. And he had that *Wisden* ...

'Toby?'

'What?' My mind had wandered. 'Sorry?'

'The Tied Test?'

'Oh yeah, well, I took Rahul back to India. To 1986 and the game in Madras where Dean Jones made 210 runs and almost died doing it. But you know what? That Brisbane game's a possibility,' I said, nodding slowly.

'Yeah?'

'What are you doing this afternoon?' I asked, helping her tip the mostly melted ice out of the esky.

Ally shrugged. 'Maybe going back to 1960 with you?' she suggested, her face brightening. 'Hang on!' She jogged over to her car, had a few words with her dad and came back grinning. 'We're on! Dad's gonna drop me around later. He's got to go and pick up my brother. About three?'

'Okay,' I said. 'See you then.'

40

George Lohmann, playing for
England against South Africa in 1896,
managed these amazing bowling figures: 14.2 overs,
6 maidens and 9 wickets for 28 runs in Johannesburg;
9.4 overs, 5 maidens and 7 wickets for 8 runs in Port
Elizabeth. He took 35 wickets in three Tests with a
bowling average of 5.80! (That's a wicket for every
5.8 runs scored off his bowling.)

5 All Tied Up

Saturday — afternoon

'IT'S got to be cooler than this in Brisbane,' Ally said, when I opened the door to greet her.

'I forgot to mention about fashion and stuff,' I said, letting her in.

'Fashion?'

'Shut the door, Tobes!' Dad called. The heat outside was like that in a furnace and Dad must have felt the temperature rise a few degrees in the kitchen.

'You know,' I looked at her, 'blending in. Not standing out in a crowd.' I paused, then shouted into the living room. 'Ally's here!' Dad was settled in watching the cricket on TV in the only air-conditioned room in the house, while Mum and Nat were shopping in comfort down at the supermarket.

'Hi, Ally,' he called, as we headed for the stairs. 'Are you guys coming in to watch?'

'Nah, we'll listen in on the Net.' I signalled Ally to follow me upstairs.

Although Mum had closed my window and pulled down the blind, it was still hot in my room. 'Maybe watching the cricket with Dad would be better,' I suggested, suddenly nervous as I stood in the middle of my bedroom while Ally hovered at the door.

'No way, stupid.' She smiled. 'We won't be here, remember?'

'That's all very well until someone comes looking for us.' I headed over to the bookshelf to find the 1962 *Wisden*.

'So, we'll just say we stepped outside for an ice cream,' Ally said, walking over to me. 'Now what's this about clothes?'

'It probably doesn't matter. We'll just have a quick visit, okay?' I thought back to India and Rahul's dramatic behaviour when he ran off to see the brother he'd never met. And then of Jay, in Hobart, trying to tell a kid the result of the game and who'd win the AFL Grand Final the following year.

'Ally, you've got to promise me one thing, okay?'

'Of course, Toby. What is it?' She looked at me expectantly.

'The trouble is, it's really easy *now* for you to say, "Sure, Toby. No worries." But when we get there, it'll all change.'

'Toby, I'm a girl. I'm totally trustworthy. Don't doubt me on this, okay? Now, what is it?' She was looking at me challengingly. I shrugged. I knew how easily it could all go wrong.

'Ally, when I say it's time to go, we go straight away. Have you got that?'

'Sure, Toby. No worries.' She grinned.

'Okay. Time will tell.' I picked up the *Wisden* and offered it to her. 'You'll have to look for the section called "West Indians in Australia". It'll be towards the back.'

Ally flicked through the book. 'Got it. Now, we want the First Test, yeah?'

'Has Georgie told you about this?' I asked. Ally seemed pretty confident with what she was doing.

'A bit,' she said. 'Here we go: page 842. Wow! They're fat books, hey?' She looked up, smiling. She was so cool about it all.

'Right. What you've got to do —'

'I know. Find a date, place or score, hopefully one that's near the end of the game.' Ally muttered to herself, her head buried in the text. 'Will any number do?'

'I think so.' I felt the familiar adrenalin and excitement surge through me with the thought of more time travel. Dad often spoke about this game; he'd only bought this particular edition of *Wisden* for this series and Richie Benaud's Aussies reclaiming the Ashes from England in 1961. Dad said that both series were awesome, especially because there'd been heaps of boring cricket during the 1950s.

'Ally, go to the scorecard. It's easy to see all the scores there.'

She gently turned the page. 'Ah, okay. So, Australia were batting at the end. Here you go.'

I followed her finger into the wash of numbers and letters spilling and swirling on the page.

'Quick,' I whispered, reaching out a hand as numbers appeared, then retreated again. 'Which one?' I breathed.

'There. Look at one of those twos.'

Sure enough, a '2' emerged from the mess and I latched onto it with all the concentration I could muster. A drop of sweat fell from my forehead and landed in the swirl beneath me. I felt the squeeze of Ally's hand as I heard her gasp.

'Two ... two ...' I said over and over — and we were gone.

We 'landed' on a hill of grass, slightly away from the arena itself. I immediately sensed the tension in the crowd, although the number of people was amazingly small. Everyone's attention was hooked on the drama unfolding out in the middle of the ground 80 metres away.

I turned to Ally. There was a look of wonder on her face. I wasn't sure how she'd react, but she didn't seem too fazed by the fact she'd just travelled back in time over 40 years, as well as more than a thousand kilometres north in the space of a few seconds. Perhaps Georgie had told her more than just a bit about the wonders of time travel. And she had taken a quick trip to 1930s England.

'Ally?'

She turned to me, her smile dazzling, and with a squeal of delight she kissed me on the cheek. 'Toby, this is brilliant,' she gasped, clapping her hands as she took in the scene around her. 'Let's get closer and watch —'

'Ally? Remember your promise?'

'What promise?'

I groaned.

'Kidding,' she said, weaving a path toward the action.

'There's Richie Benaud,' I whispered, awestruck with the thought that we were seeing Channel Nine's master commentator batting.

'What's going to happen?' Ally asked as we watched an enormously tall West Indian walk back to the top of his run-up.

'I *don't* know,' I said pointedly.

Ally turned at the tone of my voice. 'Oh yeah. Sorry,' she said sheepishly, hunching her shoulders. She turned back to the cricket, and I checked the scoreboard. The Aussies were doing okay: Richie Benaud and Alan Davidson had added over 100 runs to the total and were going strong.

'How much . . .' Ally started. 'No, it doesn't matter. I'll just shut up and enjoy the cricket.'

'Good idea.'

We watched a couple of overs. The situation was getting more tense with every delivery. Davidson and Benaud had piled on a massive partnership and the crowd was sensing that something special was about to happen. From a hopeless 6 for 92, the two batsmen had steered the Aussies to 6 for 226. They were only seven runs short of pulling off a stunning turnaround.

But then disaster. There was a shout from the pitch.

'He's run out, Toby,' Ally said. We watched Alan Davidson walk back towards the dressing room.

A man pushed past me, snacks in hand. 'Bloody awesome, isn't it, mate?' he said, and then moved closer to the fence.

One over left and seven runs to win.

'Okay, Ally. It's time,' I said, expecting some excuse from her. She didn't move. 'Ally?' I said more firmly as we watched Alan Davidson walk back towards the dressing room. He'd just been run-out by a direct hit from one of the West Indians. The people around us seemed shocked, but still confident.

'Hmm, what's that?' she said, vaguely. She was enthralled, like everyone else.

'I think it's time.'

This time Ally turned to face me. 'Toby,' she said evenly. 'I am in total control here ...'

'Ssh,' I hissed, although no one seemed to be paying us the slightest attention.

'... and we are about to see the most amazing over.' There was a dreamy look on her face.

'Ally?'

She turned her head from side to side, looking dazed.

'Ally? What is it?' I cried, alarmed, as she grabbed onto a post she had been leaning against.

'Nothing,' she sighed, shaking her head. She was looking behind her every few seconds. 'Just feeling a bit in awe of what's going on. One more over and then vamoosh, okay?' There was sweat on her forehead, and her knuckles were white from gripping the pole.

'Yep, okay. But relax.'

Gritting her teeth, Ally nodded, turning to look behind her.

I looked out to the ground. The West Indies were setting up for the last over. It was to be an eight-ball over, but three wickets going in the one over — as I knew was about to happen — was still incredible.

Australia was six runs from levelling the scores, and needed seven to win. Even though I knew the result I still felt the electric atmosphere of a close game. You often got this situation in a one-dayer, but in a Test match it was very rare for the teams to be so close after five days of cricket.

'Who's bowling?' Ally asked.

I checked the scoreboard, even though I already knew the answer. 'It's Wes Hall. He's the fastest bowler going around at the moment,' I replied as I watched him charging in to bowl. The ball hit the

Aussie batter high on the leg and they raced through for a single. The crowd roared in approval; they knew exactly what was required for victory.

Ally had her head down, one hand covering her eyes. 'Toby? I think someone's calling my name.'

It was the tone of her voice that told me it was definitely time to go. Something was really freaking her out.

'C'mon, Ally,' I said, unhooking her hands from the pole. For a moment it seemed like she wanted to pull away from me, but I hung on firmly.

Once more she turned, her mouth gaping as though she'd just seen a ghost.

> *What wonders abound, dear boy, don't fear*
> *These shimmering pages, never clear.*

I quickly said the first two lines of the poem as I pushed through the spectators and into some space away from the crowd. I heard screams and groans, and I turned for one last look at the field. Richie Benaud had just been caught by the keeper, attempting a big hit.

When we arrived back in my bedroom, Ally thanked me, though she wasn't as excited as she'd been before we left.

'I told you weird things happen.'

'Yeah, something strange *was* going on. But I'm glad I went.'

In 1972, Patrick Pocock took five wickets in six balls. He was playing for Surrey against Sussex in the English County Championships.

6 Georgie Snaps

Saturday — evening

'I'M not sure that I've ever contemplated such a fine array of food, Jane,' Jim said, beaming as he surveyed the plates in front of him.

A cool change had arrived and a fresh breeze was pushing the hot air out of the house. Dad had just walked in with a huge plate of chicken kebabs, hamburgers, prawns and lamb steaks which he set down on the table alongside the rice salad, potato salad and about five other green salads.

For a while no one spoke as we all tucked in. Ally, Georgie, Rahul, Jimbo and Jay had all turned up to celebrate our semi-final victory. And to top it all off, Mum had even allowed Dad to manoeuvre the TV so that every now and again we could get a look at the one-dayer in Sydney.

'We're very glad you're able to stay with us tonight, Jim,' Mum said, smiling at him.

'He could stay for ever,' I interjected.

'Well, it's very kind of you to have me.' Jim smiled.

I wanted to know about what had been happening at the MCC library but I wasn't quite sure how to ask. Perhaps Jim sensed my curiosity.

'It would appear that my time at the library is over, but when one door closes there's sure to be another that opens somewhere.'

'Why can't you stay there?' Jay blurted out, reaching for another kebab.

'It's called downsizing,' Jim said. 'Our friend Mr Smale ... '

'He's no friend of anyone here,' Jay said.

'Jay, can Jim finish what he was going to say?' Dad asked.

'Sorry, Mr Jones.' Jay looked a bit embarrassed.

'Well, I was just going to say that David, the main librarian, and Phillip Smale are in the process of making a number of changes, and quite frankly I'm rather glad I'm not there.'

'What sort of changes, Jim?' Dad asked, looking up from his plate.

'Well, bringing in the electronic age for a start. And he is removing all the significant works and older pieces. He's concerned about their safety.'

'Removing them to where?' Georgie asked.

'Away from the eyes of the public,' Jim said sadly.

'How dumb is that?' I spluttered. 'What's the point of having fantastic old books and scorecards and photos and cricket bats and caps and stuff if people can't see them?'

'You might as well just bury them away in a vault,' Jimbo said, shaking his head.

'Exactly,' Jim said.

'It does sound rather odd,' Mum commented. 'What does everyone else at the library think?'

'They are all somewhat swayed by Phillip Smale's offering.'

'Which is?' Ally asked.

'Which is, I'm told, the most significant and valuable collection of cricket memorabilia in the Southern Hemisphere.'

I noticed the sceptical look that passed between Dad and Jim.

Rahul let out a low whistle. 'Wow!' he gasped. 'Really?'

'Evidently,' Jim said, though he didn't sound convinced. 'Though one would think that such a significant collection would have been known and already on display somewhere by now.'

We took dessert — a choice of chocolate-ripple cake, fruit salad or a waffle cone — back into the lounge to watch the rest of the cricket in comfort, but after about ten minutes it started raining in Sydney. As a fill-in, Channel Nine put on a replay of an old game. Dad always gets excited when this happens.

'This is a cracker,' he said. 'This innings has got to include one of the best-ever one-day knocks. Do you know how many sixes Ricky Ponting hit?'

'Dad, don't spoil it,' I begged. But he'd certainly got everyone interested; even mum came in to have a look.

'You keep going in the kitchen,' Dad chuckled to her. 'I'll tell you when Ponting's innings starts.'

Mum tossed the tea towel in Dad's general direction and sat down on the couch. But we only got about fifteen minutes worth of highlights before Channel Nine switched back to the end of the live Sydney game. Still, it was great watching Adam Gilchrist and Matthew Hayden smashing the Indian attack all over the place.

Dad was really disappointed.

'Well, I'm sure the game is available on DVD,' Mum told him, heading back to the kitchen.

Dad got up to follow. 'I guess so, though what I'd give to have been there to see that game,' he said.

'Maybe Toby . . . '

'Jay!' I snapped.

'. . . could buy it for your birthday?' he concluded lamely.

But luckily Dad hadn't heard.

'Why don't you take your dad?' Jimbo asked, as the guys and I headed for the door a little later. Some of their parents had arrived to pick them up.

'Yeah. You've taken all of . . .' Ally stopped short.

I looked over at Georgie, who raised an eyebrow then lashed out.

'Well, Toby. Who else do you plan to take? Jimbo to Melbourne, Rahul to India, Jay to Tasmania, me to England. You've taken Jim and now Ally. Why don't you take the whole team on a trip to —'

'Why don't you shut up?' Jay snapped. 'Toby can take who he likes.'

'Toby can speak for himself, too,' she said, looking at me.

'I took Ally 'cos she wanted to go. She seemed to know plenty about it anyway,' I said defensively, staring at Georgie.

'Hey, what's the problem?' Ally asked, throwing her hands up.

I walked to the door and opened it. Rahul's Dad was waiting.

'Well, see you all tomorrow,' Rahul said, escaping. 'Thanks for the great night, Tobes.'

The others left soon after.

'Sorry for snapping,' Georgie said as the two of us headed back inside. 'I did tell Ally about it. She deserved to go again. I'll be honest with you; I was jealous ... I guess I wanted this to be just our special secret, you and me!'

'It always will be, Georgie.'

I told her about our trip to Brisbane, though I didn't mention Ally's odd behaviour. Georgie then left for home after we'd made plans for me to call by her house tomorrow on the way to practice.

In 1972, Australian Bob Massie took 16 wickets in his first Test match (against England at Lord's). He took 8/53 in the first innings and 8/84 in the second innings. Only four other bowlers have taken 16 or more wickets in a Test match.

7 Toby Jones Opens on Boxing Day

Sunday — morning

MR Pasquali had arranged to hold our Sunday morning practice at the Scorpions' home ground. I guess he thought it would be good for us to familiarise ourselves with the pitch and surrounds.

'Geez, I hope they're not training there too,' Georgie said as we rode to the ground. But the place was deserted, or so we thought.

As we stowed our bikes over near the clubrooms we noticed a sleek black car parked in the rear. Edging around the front of the building, we crashed into Phillip Smale, who was carrying bundles of papers.

'You,' he snarled, bending down to pick up some of the papers that had fallen. 'What are you doing here?'

'Practice,' I said, defiantly.

'Give me that!' he snapped, snatching a small card from Georgie's hand. 'I don't need your help.' He looked at both of us sternly, discreetly trying to hide the card that Georgie had picked up for him.

We all turned at the sound of Mr Pasquali's car approaching from the other side of the ground.

'You just stay clear of my affairs, do you hear me?' Smale hissed, leaning closer. Georgie and I took a step back. He spun around and walked towards his car.

I began to turn away but then sensed Georgie stiffen next to me.

'What now?' she sighed.

Smale was storming back towards us. He brushed past Georgie on his way up to one of the windows, where he ripped away the Master Blaster poster, muttered something then charged off again. He sped out of the car park a few moments later, almost colliding with a car coming in.

'Did you get a look at the card he was so stressed about?' I asked Georgie.

'It looked like some sort of business card with a website address on it,' she said. 'Nothing to get too anxious about,' she added.

'Unless he doesn't want us knowing about the site. I wonder what it was?'

Georgie smiled. 'I knew I shouldn't have looked,' she giggled.

'You saw it?'

'Yep, it was w-w-w dot scorpions dot com dot a-u.'

'Cool. We'll check it out later,' I suggested, watching two more cars arrive. 'He obviously doesn't want us knowing about the Master Blaster either,' I added.

Mr Pasquali took us through some light exercise and fielding drills, emphasising the importance of total concentration in the field. Everyone dived and darted about, knowing that there were only eleven spots up for grabs for the grand-final team. Maybe the first six spots would be filled automatically, but people like Ivo, Ally, Georgie, Jay, Gavin, Jason and Minh were all trying their best to impress Mr Pasquali with their catching, throwing and ground fielding. Damian and Trent from a lower-division team had also turned up; it was good to see them here supporting us ... though maybe they were secretly hoping for a couple of us to get injured so they could have a shot at making the team.

'Okay,' Mr Pasquali shouted, calling us in. 'Ally and Ivo, put your gloves on and meet me out in the middle. The rest of you, take a breather.'

We watched Mr Pasquali throw some short, firm catches to both of them. Ally looked as sharp as ever, catching everything that came her way. Ivo was also good, but at one stage he hurled his glove into the ground after he'd dropped one.

'Maybe he injured his hand?' Jay said, looking concerned.

'Injured his pride, more like it,' Georgie said. 'He's okay.'

Martian put his glove back on, slapped his gloves together and continued catching.

'Do you want to tell the others about the business card?' I asked Georgie quietly. Mr Pasquali and the two keepers were heading in and it looked like it was the end of the session.

'Nah. Let's see if we can find anything first. Ally's brother is a total legend with computers if we need the extra help ... You should enjoy that,' she added, smirking.

'Ally's brother?' I asked, surprised.

'No, idiot. Involving Ally.' She stared at me. I tried to look confused. 'Forget it,' she said, whacking me on the shoulder.

'Hey, are you guys coming into town to check out that virtual cricket machine?' Jimbo asked, walking over to us.

'You bet,' I said. Only four of us were able to make it. Jay and Ally were really annoyed because they had family events organised.

'Oh my God, look!' Georgie said, as we turned a corner and walked into the central square of the shopping centre. Standing next to a big sign which read 'Cricket Master Blaster' was none other than Phillip Smale. He was talking with a young guy, who appeared to be the owner or operator of the machine.

'What's Smale doing here?' I asked.

'He's probably going to buy it and keep it exclusively for the Scorpions,' Georgie grumbled.

'Or put it in a vault with all the old cricket stuff,' Rahul suggested.

'How much?' I asked. The young guy had seen us coming and moved a step away from Mr Smale, who had his back to us, apparently fiddling with something.

'We'll have a little chat later, all right, Alistair?'

But the guy, Alistair, didn't appear to hear Mr Smale. 'Hi there. It's twenty dollars for three six-ball overs,' he said. 'Fancy a hit?'

'Fancy a hit?' I repeated excitedly, reaching for my wallet.

'Well, well, looking for some extra practice, are we?' Mr Smale had turned round, no doubt recognising my voice. He had a mobile phone to his ear.

'How does it work?' Georgie asked, ignoring Mr Smale.

'Okay,' said Alistair. 'We program in your challenge and then you put this headset on and see how you go.'

'Challenge?' Georgie queried.

'You pick the bowler you're facing, your opposition, whether it's one-dayer or Test match, the ground you're playing on, the situation in the game, even the commentators you'd like to have calling your innings.'

I was licking my lips in anticipation. I couldn't wait — I knew exactly what I wanted. 'Can you buy this machine?' I asked, stepping forward with my wallet open.

'Ha, ha.' Alistair smiled. 'As far as I know this is the only one in the world, so I'm afraid —'

'Everyone has his price,' Mr Smale chuckled, but I don't think Alistair heard him.

'Okay, you want a hit?' he asked me. I pulled out a twenty-dollar note.

'Do I get a free go if I survive?' I asked.

'Let me know your challenge first and we'll see. What's your name?'

'Toby Jones. And I'm at the MCG, facing Shoaib Akhtar in the second Test match —'

'Whoa, hang on there, Toby,' Alistair chuckled, frantically feeding the data into the machine via a touch screen. Suddenly an image appeared on the huge screen. It was the MCG, and there was Shoaib Akhtar standing at the top of his run-up, his black hair blowing in the breeze as he tossed the ball from one hand to another. I suddenly felt very nervous.

'Is he really going to bowl to me?' I asked.

'C'mon, Toby. He can't actually hurt you. He's not really here in the shopping centre,' Rahul said.

'Isn't he?' Alistair said, quietly. 'You ask Toby that in ten minutes time. Okay, Toby, what's the situation?'

I'd been planning a tight finish, but seeing Shoaib standing there waiting for me made me rethink.

'Um, can he bowl off his short run-up?' I asked.

'Toby!' Rahul and Jimbo said at the same time.

'Okay. It's the first day of the Boxing Day Test match.' I swallowed. 'I'm opening with Justin Langer.

Matthew Hayden's got a stomach bug and couldn't make it.'

Alistair was typing away madly. A dull roar could now be heard coming out from the speakers behind the screen. A small crowd was gathering around us.

'Who's in the commentary box, Toby?' Alistair asked.

'Richie Benaud and Bill Lawry,' I said without hesitation.

'Okay, that about does it.' He took the twenty dollars from me and handed me a pair of batting gloves, some pads and a bat.

'What about a helmet?' someone called from the crowd, laughing.

'Yep, but not the sort you're thinking of. This one's worth just a little more.' Alistair carefully lifted a big silver helmet that looked like the one Darth Vader wore.

'Any last requests?' Jimbo said, helping me seal the Velcro ties on my pads.

I had a thought. 'What happens if I go out?'

'Guess,' Alistair chuckled.

'I go out?'

'You go out. And Australia lose an early wicket on the first day of the Boxing Day Test match.'

Now my stomach was really churning. Alistair walked me over to a patch of green where a set of stumps stood and two white lines were marked out. Ahead of me was a full-length pitch, and beyond that was the enormous screen, which was almost the size of a movie screen. I was facing away from the growing shopping-centre crowd and looking at Shoaib Akhtar standing in the distance. Boy — maybe he was getting impatient.

Alistair gently placed the helmet over my head. I could hear a crackling sound, then the unmistakable voice of Bill Lawry:

'Does it get any better than this? It is the opening day of the Boxing Day Test, and the young talent Toby Jones is out there to face the music.'

'Bill, this will be a baptism of fire,' Richie remarked in his understated way.

I swallowed again, and licked my lips. The crowd noise was electric. I could hear the Pakistani players geeing each other up and clapping their hands. This was turning out to be the most thrilling moment of my life. It was one thing to travel to Test matches; it was another thing altogether to be playing in one.

Inside my helmet I could see the same scene that everyone in the shopping centre plaza could see on the big screen. I took guard, looked around the field, then tapped my bat on the pitch, waiting for Shoaib to begin his run-up. The crowd noise became deafening. I jumped as Bill Lawry's voice came on again:

'It's all happening!'

Shoaib roared in like a train. I almost passed out as he came closer, gaining speed with every stride.

'It's just a game. You're in a shopping centre, idiot,' I muttered as he stormed past the umpire.

Suddenly a red dot was heading straight for my head. I ducked, almost falling over.

'*Oh, what a beauty!*' Bill called, delighted.

'All right for you,' I muttered, picking myself up. The Pakistani players were chatting and jumping about, supporting Shoaib.

'Keep your eyes on the ball, Toby,' Justin Langer called out, walking down the pitch.

'Justin?' I tried to say, but no sound came out.

He just smiled at me encouragingly. He pointed to his eyes, reaffirming his advice.

I settled over my bat. The noise was deafening. There was chanting and clapping as Shoaib ran into bowl. This time I watched the ball rocket past, well wide of the off-stump.

'*It's a beautiful day, Richie,*' Bill said cheerfully.

'*It most certainly is, Bill,*' Richie drawled.

I pushed blindly at the next ball. It flicked the edge of my bat but there was a great roar from the crowd. I looked around to see the ball racing away through a vacant fourth slip and down to the third man boundary for four. Then a replay was shown inside the head piece.

'*Well, it's a glorious day!*' Bill laughed. He sure was chatting about the weather a lot.

'Nice work. You kept that down well,' a voice said. Was that meant to be Justin Langer speaking?

The next ball was short, but much faster than the first three deliveries. Again I ducked, my arms and bat flailing in the air, but unfortunately I knocked my stumps. Shoaib and his team-mates raced into the middle, hugging and yelling.

I felt a hand on my shoulder as the screen went black.

'Toby?' The helmet was taken from my head and Alistair stood there smiling. 'Are you okay?' he asked.

I was a little unsteady on my feet but amazed by the game all the same.

'That was the most awesome thing in the world,' I cried, tearing off my gloves. At that moment I would have given up *Wisden*s, time travel and the grand final next weekend for a fistful of 20-dollar notes.

'Nice going, Toby,' Rahul said, grinning. 'My turn.'

I sat down to take off my pads and watch on the big screen as Rahul took guard. Bill's voice blared over the loud speakers. I turned to see a crowd of about a hundred people gathered round.

'C'mon, Rahul,' I murmured as Shoaib charged in.

Suddenly the screen went black. Alistair worked frantically on the touch screen and then on a keyboard, but after a minute he gave up.

He looked up sheepishly. 'There are still a few things that need ironing out,' he said, handing Rahul his 20 dollars back.

The crowd slowly moved away but we hung around, hoping that Alistair might be able to fix the glitch.

'There!' he cried, a few moments later. 'But there won't be any commentary. Now, who's up for one more shot? No charge.'

Georgie shot her hand up and raced over before we could get a word in.

We waited impatiently for Georgie's challenge to appear on the screen. She was chatting to Alistair and putting on her gear at the same time.

A few of the onlookers had wandered back. 'It's Lord's,' someone called as an image appeared.

'And Michael Clarke,' a girl squealed. Sure enough, Michael Clarke, with his cheeky grin, appeared on the screen. He was spinning the ball from one hand to the other and barking out instructions to the fielders.

'Remember, you promised!' Georgie said to Alistair as he placed the helmet over her head.

'Promised?' I said, turning to Rahul, who just shrugged in reply.

'Is she playing for England or what?' I asked.

'Must be. Look!' Jimbo was nodding at the batter at the other end, dressed in light blue. It was a one-dayer between England and Australia.

'Cool,' I said, under my breath.

The first ball was a slow full toss. Georgie swung it away through mid-wicket. The crowd roared as the ball raced away to the boundary for four, and then hushed as Michael Clarke walked in to bowl again. It was another full toss, exactly the same as the first. Georgie swung again, this time sending the ball behind square leg for another four.

'Look, the score's appeared,' Jimbo said, pointing to the top corner of the screen.

Australia: 7/324. England: 9/315. And only four balls left.

'She's set herself 18 to win,' Rahul said, smiling.

'And just one over to get them,' added Jimbo.

'And with Michael Clarke bowling full tosses.' I laughed. 'She's programmed him to bowl six slow full tosses at her. What a ripper!'

'*Well, surely Australia can't lose the World Cup from here,*' Ian Chappell said, sounding worried. Even the crowd behind me groaned.

Georgie belted the next three balls — all full tosses — for four. Michael Clarke stood there, his hands on his hips, looking totally shattered.

Everyone in the plaza was clapping Georgie as the helmet came off.

'You guys are such nongs! Why would you want to face up to Shoaib Akhtar when you could win a World Cup against the young blond Aussie star at the home of cricket?'

We all just stared at her.

'At least we were playing for *our* country,' I said.

'Yeah, well, that was one sacrifice I had to make so I could have Michael Clarke bowling at me. Neat about the full tosses, huh?' She slapped me on the back.

BANG!

A short, sharp explosion had everyone jumping and ducking for cover. A small trail of smoke from a big black box near Alistair drifted into the air.

'Oh, no,' he sighed, though he was grinning. 'I guess we've overworked the Blaster.'

Before we left we managed to get a card from Alistair with his phone number on it.

'Actually,' he said as he handed it to me, 'I'm not really supposed to have gone public yet, but I just wanted some kids to try it out.'

'Well, if you want a permanent volunteer for the job of testing the Master Blaster, I'm your man,' Jimbo said.

'Thanks,' Alistair said. 'I'll remember that.'

In the first over that Ralph Phillips ever bowled in a first-class game, he took a hat-trick. He was playing for Border against Eastern Province in South Africa during the 1939–40 season.

8 The Double-wicket Comp

'I didn't have any luck with that Scorpions' website,' Georgie said, as we headed to the ovals for training.

'Yeah? What was the site like?'

'Pretty normal. It just had some photos, team lists, statistics and stuff like that.'

'Anything about the Master Blaster?' I asked.

'Nope. Why?'

'I dunno. I'm just suspicious about Mr Smale being at the shopping centre, talking to Alistair and speaking continuously on his mobile phone.' I looked across the cricket ground. It was one of the few parts of the school that still had green grass; the summer had been long, hot and dry. 'I dunno,' I repeated. 'He's up to something. Plus he's got the scorecard — there's no way he'll be putting that down in his precious vault.'

'Yeah, well I gave the website address to Ally,' Georgie said. 'Her brother, Ben, is going to check it out and see if he can find anything.' She picked up an old cricket ball from the long grass behind the practice wickets.

'I looked up Master Blaster on the Net,' I said, holding out my hand for her to throw the ball to me.

'Anything?' she said, tossing it.

'Music systems, cricket bats and Viv Richards,' I told her, catching the ball.

'So, nothing about virtual cricket?'

'Nup, not a sausage.'

We went for a warm-up lap of the oval, then joined the rest of the team for some stretching. I was really looking forward to this practice. Mr Pasquali always organised a special game on the second-last practice of the season. It had become a bit of a school tradition and there were plenty of school kids, parents and teachers who had come to watch.

'Okay, people. This is the double-wicket competition,' Mr Pasquali called, coming over to where we'd gathered. 'You're probably familiar with the rules but I'll go over them quickly while you finish your stretching.'

All we really wanted to hear were the pairings Mr Pasquali had decided on, but no one spoke as he went through the rules.

'There will be six overs per batting pair, and every pair will face six different bowlers, each bowling six-ball overs. A wicket costs the batter 15 runs and also

71

means a change of ends for the batters. A wicket is worth 10 runs for the bowler. A run-out is worth five runs for any fielder and a catch is also worth five. I'll organise your bowling, fielding and keeping duties so everyone gets a fair go. And there will also be bonus points.'

'Bonus points?' Jono asked.

'They'll be awarded to anyone I see doing worthwhile things on the cricket field: backing up, supportive play, a fine piece of fielding or maybe an act of sportsmanship. That's all at my discretion.'

'And so every run is worth ... one run?' Jay asked.

'Exactly that, Jay,' Mr Pasquali replied.

'But what if my overs are against Jimbo or Jono ...'

'Jay!' about six kids exclaimed at the same time.

'It's just practice. We're a team, remember. We've got a big game on this Saturday,' Mr Pasquali told him patiently.

Jay's outburst didn't surprise me. I guess like everyone else he wanted to perform well so he'd get picked for the grand final.

'Righto,' Mr Pasquali said, opening up his blue clipboard. 'Here are the teams. Pair One: Jono and Jason; Pair Two: Rahul and Gavin; Three: Ally and Toby; Four: Jimbo and Jay; Five: Minh and Cameron; and Pair Six is Ivo and Georgie. Pair One, go and pad up. Jimbo and Jay, you're bowling first — grab a new ball from the kit and organise your field. Cameron, you're starting as keeper.

'Ripper!' Cameron said, racing over to the kit.

'Martian looks really happy,' Georgie muttered to me, sarcastically.

'Well, I'm happy. And I'd be happy swapping with Martian too,' I told her.

'Fat chance of that,' she said, jamming her cap down on her head. 'And look at Ally, all excited.'

'You and me, Tobler,' Ally called, giving me the thumbs up.

'See what I mean?' Georgie said.

Jono and Jason did a great job, knocking up plenty of runs despite Jason losing a couple of wickets. It was a similar pattern with Rahul and Gavin. Rahul must have gone close to scoring 20 himself but, like Jason, I reckon Gavin would have ended up with a negative score.

Ally and I batted fourth. Our first two overs were pretty quiet, with Rahul and then Jono bowling. But no one could complain about Mr Pasquali's organisation. The next three bowlers were not as strong and during the third, fourth and fifth overs we managed to knock up 21 runs without losing a wicket. But we were going to need a big last over to put ourselves in contention.

'Okay, we're right up there, Ally,' I said, as we came together in the middle of the pitch.

'We've got plenty of bowling and fielding points too,' she added. We watched to see who would bowl our last over.

'I reckon it'll be Cameron,' I said. Sure enough he walked across to the bowler's end, passing Mr Pasquali his hat.

'Ally, don't do anything stupid. We lose 15 runs now and we're sunk,' I said, pulling my gloves back on.

Ally blocked the first two balls and we scampered through for a single from the third. Cameron's next ball was a slower delivery outside off-stump and I swished at it. The ball clipped the outside edge of the bat and flew away over point. Jason hurled himself into the air but the ball just grazed his fingertips before racing away to the boundary for four.

'You were saying?' Ally smirked as we met mid-pitch.

'It was there to be hit,' I said. She rolled her eyes.

We scored another three runs off the last two balls, but only Mr Pasquali knew what the exact scores were as Pair Five went to put batting pads on.

By ten to six everyone had batted, bowled, kept wicket and fielded in just about every position on the field. We collected the gear and pulled bottles of soft drink from Mr Pasquali's big blue Esky as we waited for him to add up the final scores.

'Right!' he said, looking up from his clipboard. Jay passed him a bottle of iced water.

'Do I get a bonus point for that?' he asked, grinning.

'Why not?' Mr Pasquali said, making a little note on his clipboard. I looked over at Jimbo. He shook his head slightly and smiled. We both knew Jay wouldn't get a bonus point for that.

Mr Pasquali took a long drink from the bottle, slowly screwed the lid back on and put the bottle down on the grass. The spectators moved in closer, while we sat down and waited for Mr Pasquali to speak.

'That was perhaps the best double-wicket competition I've seen at this school in all my years here,' he began, looking around at each of us. 'And it demonstrated well the importance of protecting your wicket when batting — only one pair survived their six overs without losing a wicket.

I looked over at Ally, who beamed at me. Georgie was picking grass angrily. Mr Pasquali held up his clipboard, and we all crowded around to see the results.

Players	Points	Place
Jono	58	
Jason	−12	
Pair one total	46	4th
Rahul	57	
Gavin	−5	
Pair two total	52	3rd
Ally	12	
Toby	63	
Pair three total	75	1st
Jimbo	68	
Jay	−14	
Pair four total	54	2nd
Minh	9	
Cameron	35	
Pair five total	44	5th
Ivan	15	
Georgie	25	
Pair six total	40	6th

'Tobler, we would have won even if we'd lost a wicket,' Ally said, as we looked at the final totals.

'You can see all the batting, bowling, catching and bonus point scores on the sports notice board tomorrow,' Mr Pasquali said, tucking the clipboard under his arm. 'And I shall see you here at four o'clock on Thursday, warmed up and ready to go.'

'Will we be in the nets or out on the centre-wicket?' Jono asked.

'Nets,' Mr Pasquali replied. 'I've got a little treat for you.' He smiled, waved goodbye and headed over to the kit.

'Wow, I wonder what he's got in mind?' I said to Jimbo.

'I think I know,' he muttered.

'And that would be?' Rahul asked.

But I didn't hear Jimbo's answer. Ally was motioning me over to her dad's car.

'Tobler, Georgie told me about that card.'

I looked at her blankly.

'You know, the business card? The one you guys saw when you ran into Mr Smale at the Scorpions' rooms? Look!' Ally handed me her mobile phone. 'Read the text message,' she said excitedly.

I read it softly to myself.


```
hey ally, u were right, website weird,
bring yr friends over - esp Georgie -
got s'ing to show u, B
```

'Especially Georgie?' I said, looking at Ally.

'I know, weird, huh?'

'What, the Georgie bit or the website thing?' I asked.

'Nah, the website. Ben's always had a soft spot for Georgie,' she laughed.

'Yeah? How old is he?'

'Fifteen, going on 11,' Ally said. 'So, do you want to come around and have a look tomorrow night? Georgie's calling round after tea.'

'You bet,' I said, trying not to sound too eager. But before that I wanted to go and have one more look at the Scorpions' oval and clubrooms. Especially the clubrooms.

Richie Benaud — who was the Australian captain in the 1960 Tied Test — achieved the bowling figures of 3.4 overs, 3 maidens and 3 wickets for 0 runs in a Test match against India in Delhi during the 1959–60 season.

9 The Crazy Ride

Wednesday — afternoon

I left the bike at home, opting for my skateboard, which I hadn't ridden for weeks. I stuck to the pavement, enjoying the sound and rhythm of the board as it sped over the cracks in the concrete.

There was only one stretch where I had to pick it up: the dirt and gravel road that was the entrance to the Scorpions' ground. I thought of taking the path that wound its way through the cemetery that was next to the oval but I didn't want to be here for too long.

There was no one about apart from a guy jogging with his dog on the far side of the ground and an old couple heading into the cemetery with some flowers.

I walked over to the clubrooms, leaned my skateboard against the wall but decided to keep my helmet on. I placed my palms against a window and pushed to the right. Luckily it opened. Taking one last glance around, I moved the curtain aside and quickly climbed through the opening. I found myself in the main room, which I recognised from when Georgie and I had snuck in here a few weeks ago, trying to find out more about Smale.

I'd only just slid the window closed when I heard a truck approaching. I crouched below the sill, thinking that it was probably another visitor to the cemetery — maybe the gardeners. I craned my head up to look through the window and saw the truck edge past the cemetery entrance, coming towards the clubrooms. I heard it come to a stop around the corner of the building, out of sight.

I ducked away from the window and tried the door to Smale's office. Predictably it was locked and so too was another door nearby. I was just heading over to a notice board where a huge Master Blaster poster was pinned when I heard keys jangling over by the main door.

I darted back to the window, wrenched it open and jumped out, half expecting a voice to shout at me as I scrambled over the edge.

I stood still outside the open window, my back stiff against the warm bricks of the building. My heart was thumping as the main door creaked open. I carefully pulled the curtain aside a few centimetres and peered through the gap.

Phillip Smale was entering the room backwards, pulling a trolley with three silver boxes piled up on it. He struggled with their weight as he unloaded them. A few moments later Alistair followed him in, carrying a large cardboard box.

'It's good of you to look after the Blaster, Phillip,' Alistair said, putting the box down.

'It's an absolute pleasure, Alistair,' Smale said. They both headed out and I waited a few minutes, concealed as I was from the truck and the main entrance. The two of them soon returned, this time Alistair with the trolley in tow.

'Now I have something to show *you*,' Smale said as they began stacking up the boxes.

'Oh, actually —'

'No, no,' Smale interrupted him. 'You have no choice, Alistair. You've shown me the Master Blaster. I've got something even more impressive.'

'Well, thanks, Phillip, but —'

'There,' Smale continued, totally ignoring Alistair. 'It's all completely safe here, I assure you. Now come along. You were telling me about that one-day game you went to in Sydney, when Michael Bevan hit the winning runs?' Smale's voice trailed off as the two left the building again.

The truck's engine started up. What was Smale up to? I wondered. Was Alistair in trouble? I stayed hidden as the truck slowly headed back out of the grounds. It stopped at the exit, waiting for some traffic to pass.

I tucked the skateboard under my arm and sprinted down the driveway. The truck pulled out, turning left onto the street. It accelerated away, but almost immediately slowed down again. I dropped my skateboard, wheels down, and jumped on, pushing quickly with my right foot.

In no time I had caught up to the truck. Careful to stay on the left (and hopefully out of sight of Smale's outside mirror), I edged up alongside it. A bank of cars, all with their headlights on, was coming down the other side of the road; it was a funeral procession. The truck came to a halt — maybe Smale wanted to turn right? But there was no way he was going to get across unless someone let him through.

I jumped when Smale honked his horn, obviously impatient to get moving. The truck jerked forward then stopped. There was a screech of brakes, another horn blast and the sound of crunching metal and shattering glass.

The truck moved forward again, and I grabbed onto a thin pipe at the back. Suddenly I was being towed along, the skateboard wheels crunching and grinding through the broken plastic and pieces of glass that were spread all over the road.

I stole a glance at the angry and surprised faces of the people in the damaged car then concentrated on staying on my board as the truck swung right into Hope Street.

We quickly left the blaring horns behind us and raced up the street. For a moment everything was going smoothly and I had time to wonder what on earth I was going to achieve by hanging onto the back of a truck.

Then it hit a road hump and my hands flew off the pole. I threw my arms out to balance myself, crouched low and sailed off the top of the bump.

But Smale had stopped the truck. I ducked, instinctively throwing my arm out to protect my face as I smashed into the back of it. My shoulder took the force of the collision, the skateboard skidding out from underneath me and flying beneath the truck.

I lay on the road, slightly dazed, then picked myself up and ran around to the passenger side. Jumping onto the step, I opened the door. To my amazement, the cabin was empty.

Readjusting the straps of my helmet, I clambered in, desperately searching for something: a *Wisden*, the scorecard, anything to give me a clue as to what had just happened. But there was nothing but food wrappers and empty drink cartons.

I climbed back down, looking left and right. The line-up of funeral cars was still visible at the bottom of the street, crawling towards the cemetery, but Hope Street was deserted.

I dived beneath the truck and kicked my board back towards the gutter.

'When will you bloody learn?' Smale snarled, suddenly appearing as I picked myself up.

'Where's Alistair?' I asked.

'*Where's Alistair?*' he mimicked. 'Look, this is not some Famous Five adventure, you interfering little creep. Now get into the truck.' He stood over me threateningly, quickly glancing up the street.

'Where's Alistair?' I repeated.

'Oh for God's sake, he lives here.'

As Smale spoke, I glanced down at my skateboard, but he must have noticed my look and thrust his leg out just as I jammed my own foot onto the end of the board to flick it up. We both kicked it at the same time, and it shot forward, straight into Smale's shins.

I stooped down to pick it up but Smale grabbed me by the collar, swore viciously and dragged me smartly to the back of the truck. His grip was vice-like. He pushed me up the steps and I was hurled into darkness as the doors slammed behind me.

I yelled and thumped on the metal, praying someone would hear. But the street had been deserted and a moment later I heard the driver's door close.

'Alistair!' I yelled, hoping like hell that he'd noticed something from his house. But the truck lurched forward and I was flung into the side, banging my head against some wooden boards.

I stumbled to my feet and bashed away at the lock, even using my skateboard as a hammer, but the doors didn't budge. There was no way I could open them; I'd heard Smale slide bolts across on the other side after he'd tossed me inside.

A wave of panic flooded through me as I realised the situation I was in: trapped in a truck, going to some unknown destination and, worst of all, no one knowing I was here — except the weird, crazy man who was driving. Smale was probably taking me out to the edge of town, away from people. What was his plan?

The truck came to a halt; maybe we were at some traffic lights? Suddenly someone was working on the lock, and I threw myself to the back of the truck. The enclosure filled with light as the doors swung open.

'Well, Toby Jones, I always like to give someone a sporting chance. Get out!'

We had pulled over at the top of a hill, on the steep road that ran past the old cement works. A thin path snaked its way down the left side of the road, while to the right there was a steep drop. Scrubby bushes, dirt tracks, rubbish, old fence wire and discarded signs lay scattered about, all covered with white cement dust.

I swallowed. My throat had gone dry.

'Oh dear, what a silly thing for you to do,' Smale chuckled. 'And in the week of the grand final too.'

'You can't make me go down there,' I said, looking over the edge of the path. The first 20 metres were very steep before it levelled out slightly. I glanced around, preparing to make a dash for it.

'And you can think again about running away. I'll find you — you and the old man. I can make your life a misery, and I will.'

'We just want the scorecard back,' I said.

'Oh, save me. Take the drop, Toby Jones, or I will haul you off to the police.'

'What for?' I yelled, turning on him. 'I'll just tell them that you kidnapped me!'

'How about breaking into the Scorpions' clubrooms, for one?' he sneered. 'Now hop on your silly skateboard and get out of my sight.' A cool wind blew across the top of the hill.

'I'm going to sit down,' I mumbled, walking to the edge.

'Sit down, stand up — do I really care?'

I took one last look around, then slowly sat down on the board, gripping either side and rocking gently to get evenly balanced.

Suddenly Smale's foot slammed into my back. I swore loudly as I wobbled to the left, then over the top of the rise. I jerked back to the right to regain my balance as the board plunged over the precipice.

Smale's laughter faded quickly as I tore down the first section of concrete path. For a split second I thought of purposefully falling off; what were a few scratches, or maybe a sprained wrist or ankle? But within seconds my speed was so great that I knew I'd be hurt badly.

Oh, God!

I was frozen in terror as I hurtled down the steepest hill in town. The whistling of the wind and the screeching roar of the wheels being torn and shredded by the rough path drowned out all other sounds. There was no rhythm in the cracks in the pavement — there was just one crazy, frightening blur of noise as the wheels tore over the path at a million miles an hour. I held on in desperation, my fingers stiff from the tension of gripping the edges of the board so tightly. I had it balanced, but one slight stumble, one little wobble, and I'd be crashing at 40 kilometres per hour.

I screamed as I picked up even more speed on a short drop that was almost vertical. Somehow I managed to keep all four wheels on the path. There was nothing for it but to hold on — and pray.

Just when I thought the hill was never going to end, the track started to level out, weaving to the right. I leaned into the curve and the board responded, taking the bend at a frightening speed. I leaned back suddenly to the left to avoid a small rock that was sitting in the middle of the path. The board wobbled right, then left. For an awful moment I thought I was finally going over. I closed my eyes, my last thought being a desperate prayer for no major injury that would cause me to miss the grand final.

The board ran straight over an empty bottle which exploded into hundreds of shards. Some of the pieces must have jammed in the wheels, which sent out tiny splinters of glass.

By now I was totally out of sight of the top of the hill, and I was finally slowing down. I swung back onto the middle of the path and rode along for several more metres before steering the board off to the right.

Straight away I heard it — Smale was driving the truck slowly down the hill, no doubt to see what had happened.

I kicked the skateboard off to the other side of the track, and threw myself down into the dirt, lying spread-eagled. I held my breath and waited.

Pressing my face into the dust, I heard the truck

idle past, slowly, before disappearing down the street. I stayed where I was for another few moments then carefully staggered up, grabbed my board and started the tough walk back up the hill. It was long and steep but still the shortest way home.

That could have been a whole lot worse, I thought to myself as I turned at the top of the hill and looked back at the slope I'd just ridden.

'Is that you, Toby?' Mum called when I finally got home.

'Yep,' I answered, heading for the bathroom. I washed away the blood and grime, then gave Georgie a ring. I had to tell someone about my skateboard ride, and better her than Mum.

Taking 100 wickets in a season is a fantastic achievement, and Englishman Wilfred Rhodes did it 23 times! *Wisden* records that he took 4187 first-class wickets during his 33-year career, with an amazing average of 16.71 runs per wicket.

10 Ben, the Good-looking Geek

Wednesday — evening

'BEN, this is Toby,' Ally said, as we entered Ben's room. 'And of course you know Georgie,' she added.

'Hi, Toby, Georgie,' Ben said, smiling and waving us in. 'Are you guys gonna tell me what this is all about?'

I couldn't take my eyes off the setup in Ben's room. He had a massive flat-screen computer with what looked like every possible accessory you could want. There were CDs and DVDs all over the place, as well as speakers, microphones, a scanner, digital camera, printer and even what looked like a three-in-one phone, fax and copier.

'Neat, huh?' Ben was watching Georgie eyeing the room.

'You live up here 24/7?' she asked him.

Ben laughed. 'I'll give you a tour sometime.'

'That'd be neat.'

Ally broke into the conversation. 'I think Ben is running about three dodgy businesses from up here,' she said, grinning at my awed look.

'Only three?' Ben joked. 'You've been out of the loop way too long, Ally McCabe. Now shut up and check this out.'

Ben hit a few buttons on the keyboard and suddenly the Scorpions' website was on the computer screen, larger than ever. Ben cruised around the site, clicking a few links and showing us some of the scores and pictures that were posted there.

'It's nothing special, agreed?' he asked, clicking the 'Home' button.

We shook our heads, curious to see what Ben had discovered.

'But watch this!' Ben held the pointer over what to me looked like just another section of white background.

'We're watching,' Ally sighed impatiently.

'Wait on, another ... couple of seconds ... there!'
Suddenly the pointer changed from an arrow to the hand symbol. I took a sharp breath as Ben clicked his mouse.

'I had to check the HTML to verify it, but someone's put in a time-delayed hover link here that takes you away to a secret site. Check out the URL!'

'How did you find that?' I asked, amazed at his skill, or luck.

Ben chuckled. 'I'm not telling *you* my secrets, Toby Jones.'

I noticed his wink at Georgie.

A moment later and we were staring at a completely white page.

'There's nothing there,' Georgie said. 'It's blank.'

'Great minds think alike,' Ben whispered. 'That's what I thought too, George, but look closer.'

We all leaned in.

'There, down the bottom!' I cried, causing Ally to jump.

'Exactly!' Ben said. He hit a button and the faint, blurry image got slightly bigger.

'I can hardly see anything,' Ally muttered, leaning in even closer.

'And you a state softballer,' Ben joked.

'Can you make the image darker?' I asked.

'I already did. I just wanted to see if you guys could make anything of it in its original form. I copied and pasted it into a new doc. then fiddled a bit. Here you go,' Ben said, opening up a file.

'What is it?' Georgie quietly asked, looking at the new image displayed on the screen.

'That's what I was hoping *you* guys would tell *me*,' Ben said, turning round. 'Spit it out, Toby Jones. You're the one who seems to be in the know about all of this ... according to Ally,' he added, winking at Georgie again.

I was quiet for a moment, staring at the picture. I recognised it straight away. Now that it was clearer

I could easily make out an old man bent over a set of cricket stumps. You could even see his walking stick, or whatever it was he was leaning on.

'It's Father Time,' I breathed.

'It's what?' Ben asked, peering up at me.

'Father Time; it's maybe the oldest and most famous of all the symbols to do with cricket,' I said, as I stared at the old man with his long beard.

'Oh, yeah,' Ally said. 'Look, he's putting a bail back on. Maybe he's the first-ever cricket umpire?'

'What else do you know about it?' Ben asked, ignoring his sister.

'It's a weather vane,' I replied. 'You know, it tells you which way the wind is blowing. This one sits up on top of a stand at Lord's.'

'Lord's!' Georgie cried. 'As in Lord's, the famous cricket ground where I won the World Cup?'

I nodded. 'Don't ask,' I said, looking at Ally and Ben.

'Lord's — even I've heard of Lord's, the home of cricket,' Ben said. 'Well, okay. So, we've established that this is old Father Time.' He made his way back to the original website. 'Now we've gotta work out how to get in. Watch this.'

Ben clicked on the original faded Father Time image and a new page appeared, as plain as the one before. Two words stared at us:

Username:
Password:

91

'Any ideas?' Ben asked, leaning back in his chair.

'That's why we're here in your bedroom, stupid,' Ally said, straightening up.

'Bummer! And I thought it was for my good company and great looks,' Ben scoffed, pushing the keyboard away and getting up.

'Wait!' I said, hoping Ben wouldn't disappear. 'I know a few things we could try.' Everyone turned and looked at me. 'C'mon, let's think. This is Phillip Smale's site, right?'

'Yeah, so?' Ally said. 'How does that —'

'May I?' I asked Ben. I pulled the keyboard drawer back out and sat in his chair.

'Hey, make yourself at home, Toby,' he said, throwing his hands up. He moved away to sift through a stack of CDs.

I started entering some combinations.

```
Username: Phillip
Password: Smale
```

The reply wasn't encouraging: 'Your username is not recognised.'

'Does that mean you got the password right?' Georgie asked, excitedly.

'Nup. Not at all,' Ben said, walking back to us.

```
Username: Time
Password: Travel
```

The same screen appeared.

```
Username: Father
Password: Time
```

'That was a bit obvious, wasn't it?' Georgie said, when that attempt also failed.

'Are you guys going to tell me what this is all about?' Ben asked, looking at each of us in turn.

Georgie sighed.

Ben noticed our hesitation. 'Actually, forget it. Come and look at my CD collection, Georgie. Those two can work it out.'

I shrugged as Georgie followed Ben to the other side of the room.

'So, this guy, Phillip Smale,' Ally said, squeezing herself onto the seat next to me. 'He's a bit arrogant, isn't he?'

'A bit?' I laughed, turning back to the screen.

'Wants power? Wants to do things? Wants to impress people?'

'All of the above,' I replied, typing.

```
Username: Wisden
Password: Wisden
```

No.

'Just type "Smale",' Ally suggested.

'No password?'

Ally shook her head. I put it in and hit Enter. No go.

'"Smale's"?' Again, no luck.

'Try it without the apostrophe,' Ally suggested, though less certain.

'We might as well try everything,' I said as I entered 'Smales'. 'Should we be writing all these down?'

I felt Ally's hand land on my wrist. 'Georgie!' she yelled.

All four of us crowded around.

Type in your password.

'Bad security,' Ben said, hitting the back button. 'Do it again.'

I typed in 'Smales' and pressed the Enter key. The same screen appeared.

'We're halfway there,' Georgie cried.

It took another seven tries with different passwords to get in.

Username: Smales
Password: Travels

'Oh my God, Toby. You did it!' Ally shrieked.

The screen was covered in writing. Ben was obviously reading faster than the rest of us, because he nudged my shoulder.

'Toby, move — quick!' he said.

'What, Ben?' Ally snapped. 'He's the one who —'

'Hurry!'

I shrugged and nipped out of the chair.

Ben hit the Print icon and his printer sprang into action and started churning out paper. Then he closed the website.

'Ben?'

'The guy running that site might be able to trace our computer. Only five people were meant to access it, and the owner has probably been told the five IP addresses of their computers. We weren't one of them.'

I grabbed the three pages from the printer. 'Thanks for helping out,' I said, folding them in half. Ben had already seen enough.

We raced into Ally's room, leaving Ben behind to clean up the files on his computer and try to remove the evidence of our visit. I spread the printouts on Ally's bed.

Wednesday

I have now had contact from four of you. I confirm that your interest has been received. I am just waiting for acknowledgment from one of you.

Saturday

I am still waiting for one of you to sign in and confirm your interest. I must repeat: this is the only mode of communication accepted. Do not try to contact me except by the 'Submit' link above.

Monday

I am sorry to inform the fifth person — who knows who he is — that no confirmation of entry has been received and that from 8 a.m. Friday I shall make alternative arrangements to find a suitable candidate for travel.

I should also remind all of you that you are sworn to secrecy — not only now, but for life ...

Wednesday

Of course, I am being reasonable beyond all belief in allowing you fine people this once-in-a-lifetime opportunity — you will not be disappointed, I can assure you. And, naturally, your identities are being kept secret.

There was a knock on the door and a moment later Mrs McCabe appeared. I gathered up the papers, trying to look relaxed.

'Toby, your dad's here.' She looked at the three of us sitting on the bed. 'What's been happening?' she asked, with a smile.

'Team tactics,' I smiled back, waving the folded pages in the air.

'Got it all worked out, Mrs M,' said Georgie, bouncing up to her feet.

'Well, that's great,' Mrs McCabe said and ruffled Georgie's hair.

In 1978, Chris Old took four wickets in five balls when playing in a Test match for England against Pakistan in Birmingham. Unfortunately he bowled a no ball between his first two and last two wickets. On the scorer's page, Old's over read 'o w w nb w w 1'.

11 The Surprise

Thursday — afternoon

'NOTHING flashy or fancy tonight,' Mr Pasquali said crisply to us at training. 'Everything we do, we do well. Efficiency, economy, concentration: keep those three words in the front of your mind for the next two hours.'

We warmed up with a drill called 'Five 'n Alive'. Mr Pasquali had us stand in a tight half-circle and threw fast, hard catches to us. If you dropped a catch or misfielded a ball, you had to go to the end of the line on the right. If you did something special, like taking a tricky one-handed catch, Mr Pasquali might advance you one or two places to the left.

He had an old egg timer set to ring every two minutes. Whoever was the leader of the group when the timer rang — that is, the person at the far left-hand end — got five points. The next in line got four points, then three, two and one for the next three kids. No one else scored.

In the original version of the game only the top five kids stayed in after the timer went — everyone else would just sit and watch till there was a winner. No way was that Mr Pasquali's policy; he'd changed the rules slightly so that everyone stayed in, even if you never scored any points. He had us all participating as much and as often as possible.

The catches were always harder if you were one of the top five. Ally was a freak at this game, gobbling up everything that came near her — and sometimes balls meant for the person next door.

'No problems there,' Mr Pasquali grinned, indicating Ally should swap places with Martian after she'd plucked a one-handed catch from in front of his right knee. 'I've seen Ricky Ponting do exactly the same,' Mr P said. 'He wants the ball. He wants the catch. It's as if he's willing the ball to come to him. If you don't like the ball coming at you fast, then don't ever field in the slips. You'll be a nervous wreck.'

The bell jangled for the fifth time.

'Okay, did anyone score over 15 points?' Mr Pasquali asked. No one said anything. 'Over ten?' Ally and Rahul put their hands up. 'Ally? How many did you score?'

'Thirteen,' she said, looking at her hand and rubbing her thumb.

'Rahul?' Mr Pasquali asked.

'Me too, Mr P.'

'A can of drink for each of you,' Mr Pasquali said.

'What about the surprise you mentioned, Mr P?' Jay asked. We stopped and looked at Mr Pasquali, who looked at his watch.

'Another half an hour,' he said, smiling. 'Don't look forward to it too much, though,' he chuckled.

We spent another 20 minutes fielding, practising long throws and catching as well as doing short work around the pitch, including trying to knock the stumps down and backing up the wicket. It was as exciting as the first practice months ago when the season was starting and Jimbo and Ally weren't even a part of the team.

In the nets we focused on playing down the 'V' — aiming our shots in the space between mid-on and mid-off — and positioning the front foot to the pitch of the ball, head still and over the shot with bat and pad close together.

'Play the good deliveries with respect. You'll still get enough loose stuff to put away,' Mr Pasquali said regularly as he watched each of us concentrating on good defensive technique.

'Here comes the surprise!' he called a short time later, as a small white car drove up.

'Oh, way cool!' someone yelled. Everyone stopped; balls and bats fell to the ground and a dozen kids charged towards the car. A tall guy with blond hair emerged from the passenger side.

'Danny Chapman?' Georgie gasped. She'd got there first.

He removed his sunglasses and smiled.

Danny Chapman was only 19 but he was already a local legend and fast becoming a state one, too. This season he'd taken two hat-tricks, as well as 10 wickets or more three times in the local premier-grade cricket. He'd played in two one-dayers for the state, taking a 'three-for' in the second match. He was always in the local papers, being interviewed or photographed, and he'd even appeared in a TV commercial. On his day, they said, he could bowl as fast as Brett Lee.

'That's me,' he said, grinning. 'I hear you guys have a pretty important cricket match coming up this weekend.'

We all started babbling at once. Finally Danny held up a hand as Mr Pasquali joined us.

'Awesome, Mr P,' Jay cried. 'This is the *best* surprise.'

'This isn't the surprise,' Mr Pasquali said. 'Or, at least, not all of it.'

'What?' I cried.

'No, no. The real surprise is that Danny will be bowling to some of you.' Mr Pasquali tossed him a brand new cricket ball. 'Pace,' he added, nodding his head at Danny.

'P ... pace?' Jay stuttered. 'As in from the top of his run, flat-out pace?'

'They will have full gear and protection on, won't they?' Danny asked, looking at Mr Pasquali.

'Oh yes,' he said, nodding. 'Absolutely. It's school rules.'

I caught the faintest hint of a smile on Danny's face.

'Okay. Rahul, Jimbo, Cameron, Jono, Toby, Martian and Georgie, can you head over to the nets please?' Mr Pasquali said. He took the rest of the team out onto the field for some fielding drills. We were the 'lucky' ones chosen to face up to Danny Chapman.

'He won't bowl express, will he?' Georgie asked.

'Geez, I hope he does. What an experience,' Jimbo said. He hadn't taken his eyes of Danny Chapman since he'd arrived.

'No way,' I told Georgie. 'We're about to play in a grand final. How stupid would it look if half the batting line up was out with hand injuries and cracked skulls because the coach decided to make them face up to the fastest bowler in town — maybe in the state — two days before the game,' I said, hoping I sounded convincing.

'It'd be the master stroke of all time,' Jimbo said, his eyes flashing with excitement. He was already putting the pads on! 'He's too professional to hurt us. He won't bowl bouncers. But imagine how confident we'll feel against Scott Craven if we've been able to face up to Danny Chapman?'

'Are you Jimbo?' Danny asked him.

Jimbo dropped a pad in surprise. 'Yeah,' he said, shaking the hand that Danny had stretched out towards him.

'Your coach said that you were to bat last.'

'Oh, okay,' Jimbo said, looking disappointed.

Danny winked. 'That's when I'll be warmed up and at my quickest.'

'Oh, right. Excellent! Who wants the pads?'

'Are you gonna start off with a bit of spin?' Georgie asked, one hand out for the pads Jimbo was offering.

'Maybe,' Danny laughed. 'Okay, sit down for a moment, guys, and I'll give you a few tips on facing fast bowling. I hear you've got a good bowler heading your way this Saturday?'

'Scott Craven,' I muttered. The others nodded their heads, mumbling.

'Not looking forward to it?' Danny said, eyeing each of us in turn.

Only Jimbo offered up anything positive about the looming showdown.

'And therein lies your major problem,' Danny said, squatting down. 'You guys are the batters of the team. Your job is to score the runs, but you won't score anything if you don't want to be out there in the first place. Okay, this guy can bowl. Maybe he can bowl fast. But you guys can bat — you've proved that all season. You're in the final, you're up to this.'

He paused, looking at each of us closely. 'When you walk out there to bat on Saturday, you want to be going out there licking your lips in anticipation. Focus on rock-solid defence but look for runs, especially boundaries. Defy this Scott guy with good batting technique and a positive attitude. You've got to look like winners even before you start playing like winners.'

His words were stirring and the passion in his voice was evident. Danny Chapman, the town's fast-bowling sensation, maybe a future Australian fast bowler, was talking to us — the Under–13s from Riverwall. By the time he'd finished we were all bursting to get the pads on and show him what we could do.

'I'll look at your technique, but that's not going to change too much over the next 36 hours. What can change, though, is your attitude. Maybe it already has?'

'Well, I can't speak for the others, but I reckon mine's done a 180-degree flip in the last few minutes,' Georgie said.

For the next 20 minutes we took turns in the nets, facing Danny's deliveries. We hung on his every word about what we were doing well and how we could improve. Rahul needed to get his back foot positioned more effectively for the shorter deliveries. Jono had a tendency to step onto his front foot as his first movement, so Danny dug a few balls in short — not super fast ones, but they got Jono stepping back better. Cameron was told to roll his wrists more for his cross-bat shots and Georgie to hit through the line of the ball; she'd probably spend half the night in front of a mirror working on her follow-through.

'Toby, you're lazy with your back lift.' Danny had come down the wicket to talk to me. 'I think you're sometimes jamming down on the ball because you're a little late. With fast bowlers this could get you into a bit of strife.'

'Like it did with Shoaib,' I said, tossing Danny the ball that had whizzed past my off-stump. Danny was just ambling in, taking a few gentle paces, and yet he was sending round, red bullets down the wicket!

'Shoaib? As in Shoaib Akhtar?' he laughed.

'Yep,' I nodded. I told him all about the virtual cricket machine. 'I could have faced up to you,' I added, suddenly feeling a bit guilty. 'You could bat against state or international bowlers, but I wanted to play for Australia.'

'Fair enough. I want to play for Australia too.' He rubbed the ball on his trousers. 'The dream always comes first,' he added.

'C'mon, Toby. Let's have a look at you,' Mr Pasquali said, walking across to our net. I told him what Danny had said about my lazy back lift. After five minutes with Danny Chapman in front, bowling to me and Mr Pasquali behind, offering more advice, I felt like I could play anyone, even Danny Chapman at top pace!

Mr Pasquali didn't mind us all watching Danny bowl to Jimbo last. After a few early words of encouragement from Danny, their battle turned into a quiet, determined game. Jimbo wasn't there just to survive — he was actually putting a few balls away.

'Coach?' Danny called, indicating a longer run-up with a nod of his head.

'Jimbo, are you okay in there?' Mr Pasquali asked quietly.

'I'm ready,' Jimbo said, determination etched on his face. Mr Pasquali went and stood as umpire.

Danny moved back another 10 paces or so then ran in, smooth as ever.

Jimbo let the first two balls go through to the keeper then clipped the next one off his pads into the side netting. Everyone cheered when Mr Pasquali signalled four by waving his left arm around. The next ball, even quicker, smashed through Jimbo's defence, knocking over the yellow stump set. Danny eased up after that but he was still full of praise for Jimbo when they'd finished.

I spent the last 15 minutes of practice bowling while Danny watched. We worked on my outswinger and my slower ball as well as accuracy. He told me I had heaps of potential as a pace bowler, and with my batting I maybe could be a future all-rounder for Australia!

After ten minutes spent signing autographs Danny said goodbye, and we watched the white car disappear down the road.

Mr Pasquali had pulled off the biggest surprise of all time. We promised him he wouldn't have to touch a piece of cricket equipment for the rest of the season.

'But that was our last practice!' he moaned, throwing his hands up.

'You're just going to have to plan a bit better next year, Mr P,' Jimbo said dryly, sitting back and closing his eyes. He'd had the practice of his dreams. The Scorpions had their trump card: Scott Craven, bowler. But we had ours: Jimbo, batter.

Mr Pasquali smiled and looked at Jimbo. 'Even

with all the planning in the world some things just come out of the blue.'

'Like Jimbo?' Cameron asked.

Mr Pasquali just smiled.

During the 1972 tour of England, Ian Chappell took 10 wickets at an average of 10.6 runs per wicket. He topped the Australian bowling averages for players who bowled in 10 or more innings and took 10 or more wickets.

12 Who's Pixie?

Thursday — evening

AFTER tea I went up and stared at the computer. I desperately wanted to go back and look at the secret Father Time site, but was worried about what Ben had said.

It wouldn't hurt to go to the main Scorpions page, I thought, opening it in my browser. I scrolled down and left the cursor hovering over the blank area, as Ben had done the previous evening.

And anyway, my IP address was different to Ben's, so there was nothing to worry about as far as tracing the computer went, I tried to tell myself.

The new blank screen appeared and I scrolled down to the faint watermark of Father Time.

My hand paused on the mouse. I stared at the image, its ghostly lines almost invisible on the white background. Then, before I could change my mind, I clicked on the picture.

When the new page appeared I quickly punched in the username and password, then spun around to check that no one was at the half-open door. I hurried over and kicked it shut. My heart was racing.

'Toby!' Mum called from downstairs. 'Phone!'

I looked back at the screen, the page only half loaded. I sighed and closed the browser.

'Coming!' I met Mum on the stairs and headed back up to my room with the phone.

'Toby, it's me, Ally,' came the breathless voice on the other end.

'Ally?'

'I'm in. I've confirmed that I'm the fifth person and —'

'Ally!' I screamed. 'You've what?'

There was silence. Her voice was a lot quieter. 'I ... um, you know, I went into the site and wrote in that text box up at the top, saying ...'

'Saying?' I tried to make my voice sound calm. I guess I shouldn't be sounding so high and mighty — after all, what had I been about to do? Though maybe I wouldn't have had the courage to do what Ally had just done ... or was it stupidity?

'I've stuffed up, haven't I?' she said.

'Not yet,' I told her, trying to sound confident. 'Smale doesn't know who you are, does he?'

'Nope.'

'And I'm not sure he's smart enough to work out all that IP stuff Ben was talking about.' Silence. 'And even if he did, well, what have you done wrong by going into a website? I mean, you haven't broken any law, have you?'

'Exactly,' Ally said, not sounding reassured at all.

'So, what happened?' I asked.

'Well, nothing. Nothing at all. I just wrote that I was making contact. You know, that I was the fifth person.'

'Did you say who you were?'

'Of course not, you idiot. I used your name.'

'WHAT?!?'

'I'm joking,' she giggled. There was another pause. 'So what happens now?'

'How long ago did you do it?' I asked, wondering whether there might be a change on the website.

'An hour, maybe an hour and a half. Why?'

'I'm going to check the site. Don't do anything. I'll call you back soon, okay?'

'Okay, Tobler, whatever,' she sighed.

I tossed the phone onto my bed and logged back in, scrolling down to the bottom of the page.

Once again I was interrupted, this time by a gentle tapping on the door. I quickly hit the 'Print Screen' button as Jim poked his head around the door.

'Jim!' I cried, jumping up, but closing my browser first. He entered, his eyes immediately going to my small collection of *Wisden*s on the bookshelf by the window.

'Hello, Toby. I just called by to see how your father's studio is progressing. And, of course, to say hello to you as well.'

'Jim, I think we've got a problem,' I told him, offering him my seat. Instead he plonked himself onto my bed.

'Our friend Phillip Smale?' he asked, raising his eyebrows.

'How did you know?'

Jim smiled. 'An old man's intuition. What's concerning you?'

Grabbing the printed sheets from Ben's computer, I told Jim about the card we'd seen and the Internet site we'd hooked into. Jim took the pages and studied them, looking darker by the minute.

'Well, I think this needs investigating,' Jim said. 'I warned Phillip of the terrible potential for danger in playing with all of this, but he doesn't seem to have heeded my warning, does he, Toby?'

I shook my head. 'But what do we do?'

'We reveal a secret weapon,' Jim said with relish, rubbing his hands together.

'A secret weapon?'

'Pixie,' he said firmly, slapping his thighs and standing up

'Pixie?' I asked.

He nodded. 'Pixie, though by name only. She looks and performs like no pixie you will ever encounter, Toby Jones, I can assure you.'

I had no idea what Jim was talking about. 'Well, Pixie will have to get a move on,' I said to him, turning back to the keyboard. 'Have a look at this.' I opened up Word, and pasted in the webpage I'd copied. Jim walked over to the screen and read the final entry.

Thursday

```
Well now, we have confirmation from all.
Number Five, I shall arrive tomorrow
morning before 7 a.m. to deliver your
instructions. You have made a wise
decision that I know you won't regret.
```

'Well, it looks like an early start for one of us,' he chuckled, shuffling towards the door.

'One of us?'

'Toby, let me handle this one. Phillip Smale is a dangerous man. I've a good mind to alert the authorities, however I fear they'd take me for a doddering old fool who was talking through his hat. Our friend Smale is a slippery customer, but I'm not sure he's done anything illegal.'

'Yet,' I said, quietly.

'Yet,' he repeated. 'Come along, Toby. Peter sent me up to see if you were in bed ...'

'But what about the scorecard? He forced you to give that to him!'

'He did, but the less people that know about this the better. No, come along —'

'Jim,' I interrupted. 'What will you do? Who's Pixie? Can't I come too?'

'I shall follow our intrepid friend; Pixie is a car;

112

and no, you can't come too. Now, I believe you have some teeth that need attention, then it's bed.'

'Is Dad taking you home now?' I asked.

'That's right. We'll talk some more tomorrow, okay?'

Jim headed for the door. I waited a few moments, grabbed a small notebook and pencil, then followed him. Creeping downstairs, my back scraping along the wall, I listened for the sound of adult voices. They were coming from the kitchen, and I could hear the jangle of keys.

I snuck out past the laundry, sped around the side of the house and arrived at the back of the car. It was a big four-wheel drive with loads of room in the rear section. Would the car be open? I wondered. Yes! I opened the hatch a little and slipped in as quietly as possible, closing it behind me. I commando-crawled over to the enormous blue tarpaulin Dad used for tip runs and scrambled beneath it. A few seconds later I heard the front doors open and Dad and Jim get in.

The engine started. I stayed still, pencil at the ready to describe as well as I could the trip Dad was about to take. The plan had only half-formed in my head as Jim was leaving my bedroom, and even now I didn't know quite why I was doing this, but somehow I knew that Jim was too old to tackle Phillip Smale alone. If he was going to follow Smale in Pixie, then I was going to be there with him. But first, I needed to know where on earth Jim lived. Hopefully it wouldn't be too far away.

Dad broke the silence. 'He is really very fond of you, Jim.'

'And I of him, Peter. But I can't possibly impose on you like this. You are a young family. You have so many things that you'll want to do without the burden of an old man ...'

'Jim, I'm not quite sure you understand. We've all discussed this at length. Jane, Toby, Nat and I would dearly like you to join us, perhaps on a trial basis if you like — a month with the Joneses. I'm sure that would be enough for you anyway!'

'I shall indeed think about your very generous offer, Peter.'

There was silence for a while then Dad spoke again. 'You know, you and Toby have an amazing affinity ... some sort of connection.'

I held my breath, wondering whether Jim would spill the beans.

'He has a passion for cricket and a knowledge of the game quite remarkable for one so young. He reminds me so much of myself when I was his age.'

'Well, it would seem you benefit from him as much as Toby benefits from you, Jim.'

'Oh, I've no doubt about that, Peter. No doubt whatsoever.'

Their chat moved on to other things and I concentrated hard on noting down left turns and right turns, but it was difficult. Finally, after about 10 minutes we came to a stop and Dad turned off the engine.

Walk Jim to his door, Dad, I thought to myself. Luckily I heard both doors open and, very slowly, I lifted my head to sneak a look. Dad and Jim were standing by his door. It was a tiny little house, one in a row of them. There were no front gardens, just a long thin porch that connected each building. A dim light glowed over Jim's front door, but the rest of the street was dark and I couldn't see any road signs anywhere.

Before Dad returned I angled myself better beneath the tarp, leaving myself a line of sight through the back-left window. All I needed to see was a street sign or a special feature — something recognisable.

After only a minute of the return journey I got my break: a service-station with a big green and gold sign. Then it was gone. But I knew where we were.

In 1999, Wasim Akram took a hat-trick in two consecutive Test Matches against Sri Lanka. The first was in Lahore, Pakistan, and the second was in Dhaka, Bangladesh, in the final of the Asian Test Championship. Wasim Akram was named Man of the Series.

13 I'm Not the Paperboy

Friday — morning (early)

I woke up to the muffled ringing of my mobile phone, buried beneath my pillow. Last night I'd texted Georgie and told her my plan. I looked at the digital clock on my bedside table: 5.50 a.m. I swore, and grabbed the phone, pressing the 'On' button.

'Georgie?' I whispered.

'No, it's your fairy godmother. C'mon, you lump. I thought you said half-past five.'

I jumped out of bed. 'Okay. Where are you?'

'Two doors up, on my bike, freezing. Hurry.'

For the second time in eight hours I was skulking down the stairs like a burglar, then sneaking out the back door. Dad's bike and then Nat's crashed to the concrete as I tried to retrieve mine from behind them. I might as well have rung the front door bell for the sound I'd just made.

I closed my eyes, swore again and waited for someone in the house to stir. Nothing. Somewhere down the street a dog barked. I decided to leave the two bikes lying there and hoisted mine over the top. Putting my helmet on, I wheeled the bike down the driveway.

'I'm still half asleep,' I whispered to Georgie when I met up with her a few moments later.

'Then someone else must be sleep-walking too,' Georgie said, nodding towards my house. A light had just come on, and the side drive was as bright as day.

'Let's go,' I murmured, mounting the bike and pedalling hard.

'How far is it?' Georgie said, catching up.

'It'll take us ten minutes, tops,' I told her. I'd checked out the area on a map I'd downloaded from the Internet and there were a few laneways we could take to make the trip shorter.

It was cold and eerily silent. There was also a wispy fog that dimmed the streetlights.

'Hey, it's pretty good at this time of day, isn't it?' I said.

'What are we actually going to do?' Georgie asked, ignoring my question.

I hadn't really thought about that. Maybe we could sneak into Pixie, like I had into Dad's car last night, though big cars were not the first things that came to mind when I thought of Pixie.

'Here we go,' I said, ignoring her too. 'This is the service station I saw. I reckon Jim's place is straight down this street, on the right.' Somewhere ahead an engine was idling — the sound was a throaty rumble, deep and threatening.

'C'mon,' I called, speeding past Georgie. About halfway down the street was the line of houses I'd seen last night. An enormous car sat outside Jim's, shaking a bit and blasting out plumes of smoke from its exhaust.

'That's Pixie?' Georgie gasped, staring at the old car shuddering in front of us.

Jim's garage door stood open; I was amazed the car could actually fit inside it. 'It must be,' I whispered. We ran our bikes into the garage and dashed back to the car, stooping low to avoid detection. We needn't have bothered.

'I take it you'll be letting me drive,' a voice called from the front of the house. We both spun round.

'Jim!' I gasped. 'Um, well, me and Georgie, we were out —'

'Come along,' he said, looking at his watch. 'We may already be too late.'

'This is Pixie?' I asked, trying to open the passenger door.

'The very one,' Jim said, climbing stiffly into the driver's seat.

'I can't ... I can't open ...' Georgie grabbed the long silver handle with me and together we managed to open the door, which creaked and groaned.

'Better hold it while I get in,' she said, grinning as she shoved past me.

'I'm not sure when I last had passengers,' Jim said, reaching back for his seat belt.

'Maybe the 1960s?' Georgie suggested, hunting around for a seat belt herself.

'Hmm, you're probably right there.'

Georgie and I looked at each other. Maybe this wasn't such a great idea. 'Jim? Are you sure you ...' I began to say before we were both flung back against the seat as the car lurched and sputtered into action.

'It needs a bit more choke,' Jim muttered, pulling out a little lever by the steering wheel.

'Choke?' Georgie mouthed to me.

I shrugged.

Jim pulled hard on a thin stick poking out from behind the steering wheel and the car jolted again.

'Right then,' he said, gripping the wheel and staring straight ahead. 'I guess you two are wondering why you always see me in a taxi, and not in a Pixie.' Jim grinned, looking at us in the rear-view mirror. 'Well,' he continued, 'Pixie's been out of action for quite some time, but I've recently discovered mobile mechanics.'

I just hoped the mobile mechanic hadn't botched the job. Pixie certainly didn't sound well-oiled and tuned.

'Now, I take it you two are also keen to find out just where Mr Smale is heading this morning with his letter of information?'

'Er, yes,' I replied, feeling tiny on the brown leather seat, which was cold against my bare legs. I looked enviously at Georgie in her jeans. She had finally fastened her seat belt.

'And what's your assessment of the situation, Master Jones?' Jim asked.

'Well, I reckon Phillip Smale has organised five people to travel back to a game in the past, using the scorecard.'

'Just what we hoped he wouldn't do,' Georgie said.

'But knew he would,' I added. Pixie rumbled and grumbled as we waited for the lights to change.

'And now?' Jim asked, looking at me in his mirror.

'Well, we go to Smale's place and hopefully we can follow him to where he's going to hand over the letter. Then we —'

'Then we reassess the situation,' Jim said firmly. 'I take it your parents don't know you're driving across town with an old man at the wheel?'

'We didn't want to wake them, did we, Tobes?' Georgie said.

I shook my head. 'No, why worry them?'

Jim was working hard to negotiate a roundabout.

'How much further, Jim?' I asked.

'Almost there. We'll park a short distance away.' After a couple of minutes Jim pulled in behind another car.

'Which house is Mr Smale's?' Georgie asked.

'Three up on this side,' Jim said. 'I think we'll give our friend half an hour, then head back for breakfast.'

'What if he's already gone?' I asked. 'Why don't I just slip out —'

'No!' Georgie and Jim cried together.

Fifteen minutes later, having finally convinced Jim that it was time to do something, I had wrenched open the door and was darting from bush to bush. Jim had said Smale's garage would probably be locked but that I might be able to see, possibly through a window or under the door, whether his car was there or not.

Smale's house was big and modern, and a huge fence ran along the front of an impressive garden, but the gates were open. I didn't think this was a good sign, so I darted through them then crept along the side fence, avoiding some rose bushes as best as I could, until I reached the garage. The door was closed.

But just as I rested my ear against the door to see if I could hear anyone inside, it clanged and started going up. Wildly I searched for a place to hide. There were no trees or large bushes anywhere, so I belted across the front garden and hauled myself up the wooden fence on the other side. There was a three-metre drop to the neighbour's yard, but a sore foot seemed better than meeting Phillip Smale in front of his house.

I grabbed the top of the fence with both hands and gently lowered myself down, trying to reduce the distance between my feet and the ground. Letting go, I luckily landed on soft earth. I jogged back towards the road, careful to stay low.

'Oi!' a voice shouted from behind me. 'Are you the new paperboy? I said I wanted my paper delivered to the porch, here, not down in the garden.'

Smale's car was reversing down his driveway.

'Yep, right you are,' I looked around for the paper. 'Sorry.'

'It's over there,' the man growled, pointing to a bird bath on his open lawn. I grabbed his wrapped-up paper and took it up to him.

'On the porch in future, got it?' he snarled, snatching it from me.

I backed away, listening for Smale's car. It sounded as though he had backed out and was heading up the street, towards Pixie.

'Well, what are you waiting around for?' the guy on the porch asked, starting to get suspicious. 'Where are all your papers, anyway?' he said, moving towards me.

'Um, I ... I was just ... wondering ...'

Smale drove past and the mean guy gave him a wave.

I spun around. 'Okay, I'm off,' I called, running back to the pavement. Smale's car was well past Pixie by the time I started sprinting down the street towards Jim and Georgie.

'He's gone!' I panted, struggling to open the door. 'Did he see you?'

'We hid,' Georgie said. 'You?'

'Nup, don't think so.'

Pixie's engine grumbled deeply as it warmed up. Slowly Jim wheeled her around to face the other way, but he couldn't do it in one turn and had to reverse before heading off.

'C'mon Jim, floor it!' I yelled, doing up my seat belt.

'Hold on!' he called. Pixie quickly picked up speed and we charged back the way we'd come.

'There!' Georgie called, looking out her window. Jim hauled on the wheel and we spun to the right. I looked at Georgie, who had turned a bit pale.

'Don't worry. I did an advanced driving course some years ago, and you never forget these things,' Jim chuckled, a gleam in his eye.

We managed to stay a good distance behind Smale's sleek black car. A few times Jim backed right off and twice I thought we'd lost him, but Jim seemed to know what he was doing and a moment later there was Smale's car, 50 metres ahead.

'Ally lives around here,' Georgie said as we turned into a street with big trees along each side.

'And I think our friend does too,' Jim said, slowing down and carefully parking a safe distance from the black car's position. We watched Smale march up to the door and knock. Nothing happened.

'Did Ally choose this address?' Georgie asked, as Phillip Smale glanced about furtively.

'Nope. She just made contact. This must be the house of the fifth person,' I said, 'but no one seems to be home.'

As I watched, Smale became more and more frustrated, slapping an envelope against his thigh. Again he banged on the door, this time with his fist. Finally he left the front of the house and walked around the side. A minute later he reappeared, but without the letter.

'He must have found someone,' Georgie said.

'Time to go,' Jim said, reversing Pixie.

'But Jim, what about . . . '

'All in good time.' Jim launched Pixie back onto the road. We turned and headed up a side street where we waited for a few minutes, before crawling back to the mystery house.

This time we all got out. Jim hung back, pottering about near the front while Georgie and I dashed down the side. It was Georgie who found the letter, with a hastily scrawled note written on the back, under the doormat at the rear of the house.

'Right then, detectives. That was a successful mission, wouldn't you say?' Jim beamed as he took the letter from Georgie and we hurried back to the car. 'We shall reconvene this afternoon — at your house, Toby.' It appeared that Jim was going to get first look at Smale's letter. That was fair enough, since it was his Pixie that had brought us to it.

'Why do you call the car Pixie?' I asked, settling back in the enormous seat.

'Maybe it's got something to do with its size?' Georgie said, rolling her eyes.

'But this car is a monster,' I replied.

'Exactly,' Jim chuckled.

Charlie Turner holds the record for the most
first-class wickets in an Australian season. Playing
for New South Wales and Australia in 1887–88,
he took an incredible 106 wickets in only 12 games.
That's an average of almost nine wickets a game!

14 Timeless Travel Tours

Friday — afternoon

'THE letter is on your bed,' Jim whispered to me in the kitchen that afternoon, a few minutes after Georgie and I had arrived back at my home from school. No one had missed us that morning and there'd obviously been no calls from Mr Smale or his neighbour about any funny things going on. Georgie and I grabbed a snack from the fridge and raced up to my bedroom.

I'm pleased that you have made contact, Geoff. We shall depart from the Scorpion clubrooms at 9.00 p.m. this Saturday. We shall be gone no longer than an hour. I trust that you have been, and will continue to remain, fully discreet in this matter.

Please wear comfortable, light clothing as befitting an Australian test-goer of the 1960s.

Phillip Smale
(Manager)
Timeless Travel Tours

'It doesn't say much,' I muttered, handing the letter over to Georgie.

'No, only where and when Smale is planning his little tour party,' Georgie said sarcastically. 'What did you expect?'

'I dunno.' I was starting to get nervous about the final, worried that I hadn't been thinking about it enough — though maybe that was a good thing. Probably the more I thought about it, the more worried I'd get.

'Georgie?'

She looked up sharply, noting something in my voice.

'We've got the grand final tomorrow. I reckon we should forget about this for a bit and, you know, focus on the game tomorrow. Do you want to set a field or maybe work out a batting order?'

Georgie folded the letter. 'Yeah, Toby. Good idea.'

We spent the next hour working on fielding positions and the batting order. I'd come up with a 6–3 fielding set up: six fielders on the off side and

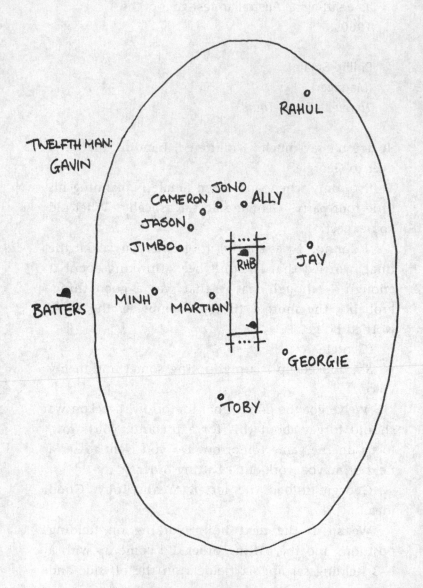

RAHUL

TWELFTH MAN:
GAVIN

CAMERON JONO ALLY

JASON

JIMBO

RHB JAY

BATTERS MINH MARTIAN

GEORGIE

TOBY

three on the on side. We could use it when I was bowling to a right-hander — though not necessarily to Scott Craven. The field would have to be spread more when he was batting.

Georgie and I had a long argument about Martian's position at silly mid-off. I would also have really liked to have a short leg, like they do in the Tests, but in our games no one is allowed to field closer to the batsman than a half-pitch length, unless you are the keeper or in the slips or gully.

'You're giving away runs down through third man,' Georgie argued, pointing to the big open area behind the slips.

'Well, if I'm finding the edge of the bat then that's good. With those two slips and a gully I might be getting a few wickets.'

'Not if their shots are going along the ground,' she replied.

'But I'm still finding the edge.'

'We might only have a few runs to play with,' she said, folding her arms.

We were going around in circles

We finally agreed that the fielding positions depended entirely on the situation of the game. Maybe at the start of the innings, when we were on the attack, we could have this sort of field.

'Yeah, but what if we'd been bowled out for only 53?' Georgie said, as we headed into the kitchen for some food.

'We still attack,' I said loudly. 'Like Danny said: we've got to look and play like winners, whatever the situation.'

'He didn't say that —'

'One more sleep to the final, guys,' Dad called out from the next room, hearing us in the kitchen.

I grabbed a couple of nectarines from a bowl on the kitchen table and headed into the lounge. Georgie followed me in.

'Cup of tea, Jim?' Dad asked, passing us in the doorway.

I noticed Jim was also in the lounge, reading a book. 'We're going to focus on the game this weekend, Jim,' I explained, passing him the envelope with Smale's letter inside.

'Good, good,' he nodded, closing his book. 'An excellent decision. The last thing you need is this sort of distraction.' He slipped the letter into the inside pocket of his jacket.

'Will you be doing anything?' Georgie whispered to Jim as I gave her a nectarine.

Jim looked at me. 'Perhaps I'll go and have a talk with Phillip, though I fear his heart is set.'

'We have to get the scorecard back,' I said.

'Not yet, Toby. You have other cricket matters to attend to. Let's think about all of this after the weekend — after the grand final, hmm? What do you think?'

I looked at Georgie. She shrugged, looking thoughtful.

* * *

Four more people were finding out about the time travel, I thought as I lay in bed trying to sleep, wondering where Mr Smale was going to take the group that had signed up for his trip.

How many people knew about it now? Me and Jim. Then Georgie, Rahul, Jay, Jimbo and, of course, Ally. Also Scott and his uncle, Phillip Smale. Maybe Gavin, Scott's friend — and who knew how many others Scott might have told?

And now four complete strangers. Four adults. What would go through their heads when they were transported back through time to a cricket match in the past? They would freak out completely. There was no way they would be able to keep that sort of experience secret.

In a week's time it could be all over the town. All over the news. On everyone's lips. But Mr Smale didn't want that. He wanted secrecy. To what lengths would he go to ensure that time travel by means of the scorecard and the *Wisden*s remained a secret?

I glanced at the red numbers on the clock next to my bed: 10:34. In ten hours I would be playing in the most important game of my cricket career and here I was lying in bed worrying about Phillip Smale, *Wisden*s, scorecards and four complete strangers about to go on the journey of their lives.

I bet Scott Craven was sound asleep, dreaming of cartwheeling stumps and high fives ...

131

The most balls bowled in a Test match by one
bowler is 774 by Sonny Ramadhin of the West Indies.
Playing against England at Birmingham in 1957,
he bowled 31 overs in the first innings, taking 7 for 49.
In the second innings he bowled a whopping
98 overs, taking 2 for 179.

15 Collapse

Saturday — morning

IT was another warm day. There were already plenty of people about when we arrived at the ground, setting up rugs, portable chairs and even barbecues.

'Finals atmosphere, son,' Dad said, looking excited. 'Come on, Nat. Help me out with all this gear. Toby,' he said, looking at me and holding out his hand. 'Best wishes, mate. Enjoy yourself. The result will look after itself.'

'Thanks, Dad,' I said, feeling nervous. I got a kiss from Mum and Nat, who also wanted to shake my hand.

Jim also gave me a handshake. 'I'm looking forward to the game, Toby. But remember, that's all it is — a game. A wonderful game, perhaps the greatest of them all, but still just a game.'

Mum, Dad, Jim and Nat watched me head across to the team area. I turned around once, halfway across the oval with my cricket bag hanging over my shoulder, and waved. They all waved back.

'We're batting,' Jono called, walking over to the team from the coin toss in the middle. I felt a tingly feeling in my stomach, especially on seeing Scott Craven warming up off a run-up that took him almost to the boundary line.

Positive, stay positive, I told myself. 'Great day for batting,' I said.

'Who won the toss, Jono?' Rahul asked.

'Scorpions.'

I looked over at Mr Pasquali for a reaction, but he was writing something into his scorebook.

'Jono, bring everyone over to the small scoreboard here, please, and I'll announce the team. Then you can read the batting order. After that I'd like you all together for the team photo and a quick chat, okay?'

All twelve of us, the squad Mr Pasquali had announced and introduced at our school assembly, followed him across to where a big magnetic scoreboard leaned against a wooden table that the scorers would use. One of us would also be sitting there, watching, ready to field if one of the team got injured.

Gavin, Georgie, Jay, Jason and even Ally and Martian would all be feeling nervous right now. No one spoke.

'It's been a long and successful season, regardless of what happens today and tomorrow,' Mr Pasquali said, rubbing sunblock into his arms. 'I said last week that you were a fine team. We agreed at the start of the season that you were happy for me to pick the in-form twelve for this game, and that's what I've done. Unfortunately, I have been faced with the difficult task of appointing one of you as twelfth man, or woman, as the case may be.'

I glanced at Georgie. She was kicking at something and avoiding all eye contact.

'I wish it was a game for twelve or even fifteen players. But it's not — cricket is played between two teams of eleven. And this is the team of eleven that will take the field in this year's grand final.'

Mr Pasquali paused, looked up at us, then down at his clipboard again.

'Jono: captain. Toby: vice-captain.'

A shiver swept through me, this time of excitement. We'd never had a vice-captain before.

'Then in alphabetical order by first name, because that's how I know you all ...' Poor Mr Pasquali was finding this difficult. He hated the thought of someone missing out. And someone was about to not play in a grand final. He looked up. 'Ally, Cameron, Gavin, Georgie, Ivo, Jason, Jimbo, Minh and Rahul. Jay, you are our twelfth man for this game.'

Jay was making a brave effort to hide his disappointment. Georgie, Martian and even Gavin weren't showing any signs of delight, though each would be feeling relieved.

Jono stepped forward into the circle. 'It's pretty well the same as last week,' he said, unfolding a piece of paper that he'd pulled from his pocket. 'Cameron and I will be opening, then Jimbo, Rahul, Toby, Martian, Georgie, Minh, Ally, Gavin and Jason.'

We turned back to Mr Pasquali.

'We have all the time in the world. I will be very disappointed if there are any run-outs or wasted wickets. But keep the runs ticking along, let's not get bogged down. If the top order can see off Scott Craven, then I'm sure there are plenty of runs for the taking. Remember, there are no limits on batters or bowlers in a grand final. *But* we have to win the game. The Scorpions finished on top of the ladder so a draw is good enough for them to win the cup.'

I tossed a few deliveries at Cameron then went over to console Jay who was sitting at the scorers' table with the Scorpions' twelfth man and a couple of parents.

'You're a part of this team, Jay, and you'll be with us for the celebrations after we've won too,' I said, patting him on the back.

'Yeah, whatever,' he mumbled, not looking up.

'C'mon, Jay. At least you don't have to face Scott,' said Georgie, who had joined us.

'You wanna swap then? Here, you sit on your arse here and do nothing —'

'Hey, young feller,' one of the men at the table said, 'that's no way to talk. As it is, you've got your part to play. Now, let's get this batting order into the book.'

I walked around to my usual spot, right behind the bowler's arm to watch the start of the game. For a moment I was the closest person in the world to Scott Craven at the top of his mark.

'Good luck, Scott,' I called, sitting down on the bank.

He turned around and looked at me in amazement. 'Well, Toby Jones,' he drawled, 'luck doesn't come into it, mate.' He sniggered, spun around and headed off to bowl to Cameron.

We survived the first five overs before disaster struck. None of us expected the other opening bowler to do much damage; maybe our batters were a bit too relaxed when Scott wasn't bowling.

First to go was Cameron, caught at mid-off by none other than Scott Craven who hurled the ball high into the air. Then Jimbo went, caught off the last ball of the same over, and I was making my way back to the group to put on my batting gear.

'C'mon, Rahul,' I called. 'Big knock from you.' At least give me time to get my gear on, I thought to myself, watching him stride out onto the pitch.

Jason managed to toss me a couple of balls before there was another shout from the field. Scott Craven had just got his first wicket, clean-bowling Rahul. We'd lost three of our top four batters in the space of about six deliveries.

I hadn't thought I'd be walking out to the middle so soon, and I felt flustered with the rush and the panic that had come over the team. Taking a few deep breaths to try and calm my nerves, I arrived at the wicket and paused to adjust my pads and tighten my gloves.

'Take your time,' I muttered to myself.

'Come on, Scott, let's have him,' a voice called.

I glanced up to see Mr Smale pacing about down near the third-man boundary. I turned away quickly.

I had one ball to face to see off Scott's over. I expected a bouncer and was ducking almost before he'd bowled it. The ball flew past my head.

'Toby, I don't care how slow we go, we've just got to survive, okay?' Jono said when we met mid-pitch at the end of the over.

'Okay. Just don't shield me from Craven,' I said over my shoulder.

'I have no intention of doing that,' he replied.

We survived the next six overs without too much drama, though Scott beat me twice in a row with two beautiful deliveries that moved away from me. After the second one, he came down the wicket a few paces and mouthed some swear words in my direction. I turned my back on him, just like some of the international players do when the heat is on.

I looked out past square leg to see Dad chatting excitedly with Jim, who was nodding as though in agreement. I then gazed at our players — they all looked a bit dejected with the way the first hour had gone. The scoreboard read 'Riverwall 3/38'.

'It's better than 3 for 19,' Jono said at our first drinks break. Mr Pasquali watched from a distance. He was chatting politely to the other umpire but inside he would be feeling the disappointment.

Scott continued bowling after the break. I played his first two deliveries back up the pitch. He'd slowed down a fraction; maybe he was beginning to tire. His third ball, however, spat and flew from just short of a length. I fended it off my body. A short leg would have gobbled it up. Scott stood and stared, shook his head slowly and wheeled around.

'Stay focused, Toby,' Jono called from the other end.

'Stay alive, more like,' I muttered, tapping the crease.

The next ball was shorter. I was inside it in a flash, flaying it high and wide over deep backward square leg. I didn't even leave my crease. Car horns blared and the umpire raised both arms. I presumed Scott was glaring at me, but I ignored him and walked up to get a pat on the back from Jono.

Scott bowled another short one, though this time further outside the off-stump. But I was on fire. Again I tried to get inside the line, but the ball was onto me too quickly. It caught the top edge, flew over the slips and down to the boundary for four.

Ten runs in two balls. I stole a glance at Mr Pasquali out at square leg. Slowly he raised a hand. *Don't get carried away*, he seemed to be saying.

Where would Scott pitch this last delivery? Would it be another short one? I heard some clapping from the Riverwall supporters as he steamed in and bowled a fast in-swinging yorker. I jammed the bat down on it. Bat, ball and pitch all collided. The ball stopped dead and I kicked it away.

The umpire called the end of over and I headed up the pitch.

'I want one more,' Scott yelled at his captain, who was standing in the slips. He got his extra over. Jono glided the first ball down through the gully for a single and then I was clean-bowled with the next delivery. I hardly even saw it.

We had been five balls away from seeing out Scott's first spell and I'd blown it. I walked off the ground dejected and angry. I didn't speak to anyone and no one attempted to talk to me. I didn't care that I'd been bowled by maybe the best ball of the match so far. No ball is too good once you've spent some time at the crease, once you've nailed a few in the middle and hit the boundary two or three times.

Martian top-edged Scott's fourth ball over slips for six, but was caught in the gully on the next ball, fending off another short one.

Georgie survived Scott's last ball, but was out lbw for a duck in the next over. Three for 38 had turned into a disastrous 6 for 55.

How could you stay positive in a situation like this?

Tom Veivers holds the record for the Australian who has bowled the most balls in one innings. Playing in a Test match against England at Manchester in 1964, he sent down 571 deliveries. He bowled 95.1 overs, 36 maidens and took 3 wickets for 155 runs.

16 Out of the Blue

WE scrounged another 39 runs off the Scorpions' other bowlers. 'Extras' ended up being the third top scorer with 13. It was easy to see how frustrated Scott felt at not being able to bowl at our lower order. Perhaps the Scorpions' captain was being a bit generous in holding him back.

'I think the Scorpions have made their first mistake,' Mr Pasquali said, smiling as he threw a ball at us at the changeover.

And with that comment our whole attitude changed.

'Taking Scott off?' Jimbo asked, flinging the ball to Ally, who would be keeping.

'Exactly,' Mr Pasquali replied.

'The ball's doing quite a bit out there. Tight, accurate bowling will be rewarded, I assure you.' Maybe Mr Pasquali was just trying to get us to be positive. So what? It was working.

Jimbo nudged me and nodded towards a guy standing on his own 10 metres away to our left.

'It's Trevor Barnes,' I whispered. 'Coach of the Under-18 representative side.'

'The very same,' Jimbo said quietly.

I took the new ball and went out to measure my run-up. I thought back to Danny Chapman and the chat we'd had. The Scorpions hadn't had that experience. Surely that was an advantage for us?

But it wasn't Danny Chapman with the ball. It was Toby Jones. And that was going to be just as good, I thought, looking around at the field Jono had set. I'd shown him my plan and he was happy to go with it — for the first few overs, anyway. Like Georgie, he was nervous about not having a third man.

'Minh, go closer to point,' I shouted. I also directed Martian to go a bit squarer from his position at silly mid-off. That way I had opened up a nice gap through mid-off to tempt the batter into driving at a ball that was either swinging away or not at a length full-enough for driving.

'C'mon, Toby, go right through 'em,' a voice I didn't recognise yelled from the boundary. I didn't turn around.

'Play,' Mr Pasquali called.

I ran in hard, looking every bit like I was going to bowl the fastest possible delivery. Halfway to the wicket, though, I spread my fingers on either side of the ball. It was the perfect slower ball, straight and pitched fuller. The batter's eyes lit up, but he was into the shot way too early. He had already completed his stroke when the ball hit the bat. Gently the ball ballooned back towards me.

I took it in both hands at knee height. The batter banged his bat into the pitch and walked off, staring at me, while my team-mates all rushed in to celebrate.

'I thought you were a pace bowler,' Rahul said, high-fiving me.

'Not all the time,' I replied.

'Body language, everyone,' Jono said, clapping his hands. He wanted us looking confident and in control.

'Game on,' I whispered to Georgie as we headed back to our positions. She was at mid-on.

'It's not the only thing on,' she said, winking at me.

'C'mon, Toby!' Jimbo shouted from the gully, clapping his hands.

I let Georgie's comment slip through to the keeper — I didn't want any non-cricket issues getting in the way and distracting me.

I took a wicket in my third over, then another in my fourth. The moment we'd all been waiting for arrived when Scott Craven marched out to the crease. The whole team stared at him as he took guard from Mr Pasquali, calling for two legs.

'One more over?' Mr Pasquali called over to the other umpire, who looked at his watch, then nodded.

What would Scott do with one over to survive before lunch?

I brought Georgie and Minh in closer, hoping to tempt Scott to go over the top. The plan worked — sort of. I should have known better. Scott carved the first two balls over Minh's head and out to the cover boundary for four each. He clipped the third off his pads for a two. The fourth ball went right through him, but he belted the next back over my head for another four. The last ball he blocked. He'd just belted me for 14 runs.

'C'mon, guys,' Jono urged as we walked from the field for lunch. 'We're only one wicket away from being level if not ahead in this game.'

He was right, but Scott Craven was a big wicket. The scoreboard had the Scorpions at 3/36 and we were only 58 runs ahead. Splitting up, we headed over to our respective families for food and drink.

Jono gave me two more overs after lunch. The Scorpions had changed their tactics — they were obviously waiting for me to finish my spell, like we'd waited for Scott to finish his.

Slowly and steadily the Scorpions started to accumulate runs with first Jono and Rahul bowling, and then when Jason and Gavin came on.

It was the hottest part of the day and we were struggling, but Scott and his partner had taken their score from the 20s into the 120s without too much sweat or bother.

'Maybe we should try and buy a wicket,' I said to the team at the drinks break.

'Buy a wicket?' Ally asked. 'You want to bribe Scott Craven?'

'No, let's set him up. He's itching to put one away; so is the other guy. I reckon they've been told to grind us into the dirt.'

'Toby's right,' Jono said. 'We've gotta try something different. It's not happening for us at the moment.' He glanced at the scoreboard. 'They're 30 odd runs ahead and putting us out of the game. Remember, we've got to win.'

'What exactly did you have in mind, Toby?' Jimbo asked. He sounded positive.

'Give Georgie a bowl. She's accurate and can mix up her pace a bit.'

'She'll get pasted,' Martian said, shaking his head. 'No offence, Georgie, but you're up and down — no spin or movement.'

'Exactly! So they get lulled into doing something stupid.'

'Or get lulled into belting her over the boundary line,' Martian said dejectedly.

'Jono?' Rahul said, looking over to him.

'That's time, boys,' the Scorpions' umpire called.

'Okay. We'll give it a try. Two overs and then we'll review. Georgie, which end do you want?'

'Into the breeze,' she replied; pointing to the far end. 'Bloody ripper idea, Tobes,' she said, clapping me on the back.

'Thought you'd approve.'

The Scorpions pair played out Rahul's next over, taking only a couple of singles. Scott was on strike for Georgie's first ball, and I watched his face closely. He was looking smug, yet determined. He would hate to get out to Georgie. He padded her first ball back down the pitch.

'Bowled, George,' Ally said, clapping from behind the stumps.

'Right there,' Jimbo called from covers.

But Georgie's next ball was short and wide. Scott leaned back and hoicked it from outside his off-stump over mid-wicket. The ball landed just inside the boundary.

Jono told Minh to drop back from his position at mid-wicket. Scott watched lazily, chewing his gum and smiling. He put the next ball out over cover. Same result.

Now the field was spread. I didn't think Scott was interested in singles, and I was right. He blasted the next ball wide past mid-on. It produced four more runs, but the shot lacked control.

'On your toes, everyone,' I shouted, clapping my hands.

'Settle,' I heard the Scorpions' coach hiss through clenched teeth from his position at square leg. Scott looked towards him in surprise.

I made a quick movement of my hand to Georgie when she turned to look at me. 'Faster one,' I mouthed.

This one was onto Scott much quicker. He slashed at the ball, which was delivered short and outside off-stump, aiming to belt it over mid-wicket again. But instead, the ball shot directly into the sky.

'Mine!' I screamed, sensing it was coming in the general direction of square leg.

'Leave it for Ally!' someone called.

'*Mine!*' I yelled again. The ball had only just reached its peak. Time stood still. My mind went blank as I stared into space at the little red dot, now hurtling back towards me at alarming speed. I squinted. I was too far forward. I took a step back, then another, then staggered three more paces.

I reverse-cupped my hands in front of my face. Still edging backwards, I caught the ball, then stumbled and fell over. I clutched the ball to my chest, closing my eyes in delight and relief.

'Told you it was a good idea,' Martian said, grinning.

I was hauled to my feet and we jumped about like galahs for a few moments before Jono held up his hands.

'We're in this game,' he roared at us. 'Two more wickets before tea, okay?'

We got him three. I came back on to bowl and snapped up Scott's partner, lbw, with a fast yorker that got him on the toe. Then Rahul got a lucky break when their number six batter played on. The ball spun back and clunked into the base of his off-stump, just dislodging the bail.

The Scorpions were rattled. Jimbo swooped on a ball played into the covers in the last over before tea. The batters stuttered and stumbled. 'No!' the non-striker finally shouted, holding up an arm. But the batter had committed. He turned and tried to regain his ground, but Jimbo's flat and awesomely fast throw to Ally caught him well short.

The dismissed batter flung his bat into the stumps in anger and frustration, and swore at his partner. Ally was lucky as the bat missed her by centimetres.

'Nicko, here — now!' The Scorpions' umpire demanded.

We went to tea a much happier group, though we could hear shouting from the other team's clubrooms during the tea break. I assumed the coach was getting stuck into them again.

By contrast, Mr Pasquali was quiet and friendly. He spoke to us individually, encouraging and giving each of us something to focus on for the next session.

The Scorpions' last three wickets put on about 40 runs, though, which was a bit disappointing. We dropped two catches during that last hour and I had what looked like a plumb lbw decision turned down too. The batter shouted straight away that he'd hit it, but it was unlikely that Mr Pasquali was influenced by that call.

We left the field as a tight group at the end of the innings. The day wasn't quite over for us, especially for our openers Cameron and Jono who would have to face a very tricky three overs to see out the day.

Padded up and ready to go in, I sat down to watch the action and see if we could get through the overs without losing a wicket. We'd already decided that we wouldn't risk Jimbo going in tonight, so I was given the role of night watchman — the batter whose job it is to go in if someone gets out, and survive till stumps.

They almost made it!

Jono was given out lbw to a Scott Craven yorker — a vicious and amazingly fast ball that smashed into the bottom of his pads. Jono was trapped in front of his wicket, absolutely plumb.

That left me with three balls to face from Scott Craven.

'Survive, survive,' I said to myself as he ran in to bowl. The first ball whizzed past my off stump. Scott threw up his arms and screamed in anger and disbelief. Maybe it had been closer to my stumps than I thought.

Two balls to go.

The next caught the edge of my bat and flew towards second slip. I spun around to see the guy thrust out his left hand. The ball bobbled, then dropped to the ground as he rolled over. To my amazement he jumped back up, shouting and holding the ball up for all the world to see.

I didn't move. Scott charged down the wicket yelling in delight. I looked over to Mr Pasquali, who'd swapped positions to be at square-leg for our innings, and gently shook my head.

'How's that?' Scott yelled, turning to the Scorpions' umpire.

I'd never felt so sick in my life. 'Don't do it,' I muttered.

The umpire looked over at Mr Pasquali, obviously not sure about the catch.

'That was not a catch,' Mr Pasquali said firmly. 'The ball hit the ground.'

'Not out,' the Scorpion's umpire called.

'What?' Scott said, looking dumbstruck and pointing to the fielder with the ball. The umpire was unmoved. Slowly the players returned to their positions, swearing and muttering.

I settled over my bat and waited for the last ball of the day.

'Cheat,' one of the kids mumbled behind me. I straightened up and pulled away from the wicket.

'Is there a problem?' the umpire asked. He obviously hadn't heard the comment.

'Just a bit noisy down here,' I yelled back. I glanced at Mr Pasquali. He smiled and gave a slight nod.

Scott charged in and bowled a bouncer. Surprise, surprise.

I ducked, but hardly needed to because the ball soared over my head as well as the keeper's and flew to the boundary for four byes. It didn't matter how the runs came, as long as they did.

In 1997, Glenn McGrath took 8 for 38 in a Test match against England at Lord's. His bowling figures for the first innings were 20.3 overs, 8 maidens, taking 38 runs for 8 wickets. These are the best bowling figures for any Australian at Lord's, and the fourth best innings' figures for an Australian.

17 Ally or Jessica?

Saturday — evening

'TOBY, we have a plan,' Georgie said excitedly.

'To stop Scott Craven taking all 10 wickets in the second innings?' I asked, just as Mum brought in a plate piled high with hamburgers stuffed with lettuce, onion, cheese, tomato, egg and sauce. She then disappeared outside where the adults were having drinks, while Ally, Georgie, Nat and I blobbed in front of the TV, ready to tuck in. Somehow I knew that the plan Georgie was talking about had nothing to do with the grand final.

'Ally did some checking out. She knows the people in the house that we went to with Jim. You know — to get that letter?'

I looked over at Nat, who was nibbling on her hamburger and feeding the odd bit to an army of Beanie Bears she had propped up against the couch. She wasn't listening to us.

'Who are they?' I remembered that Ally lived close to the area where Jim had driven us when following Smale.

'Well,' Ally said, putting her plate down, 'I don't really know them, only to say hi. Their name is Walters. They have a girl a few years older than me, called Jessica. The weird thing is they're on holiday.'

'How do you know that?' I asked, taking a bite.

'Their neighbours are collecting their mail.'

'And how do you know the neighbours are collecting their mail?'

Ally sighed. 'Because Henry lives next door to them and we often walk to school together.'

'You and Henry?' I asked.

'Is there a problem, Toby?' Georgie asked, frowning.

'No,' I said. I was still on a bit of a high after the day's play, and I would rather have talked about the fake catch or my catch to get rid of Scott, our decision to give Georgie a bowl or the state of the game.

I shrugged. 'Okay, so what's the plan?' I'd made a conscious decision, along with Jim, to put the time travel issue to one side while the grand final was on. It was after all, only two days of my life. But the girls had other ideas and their energy and enthusiasm was grabbing my attention.

'We think that the father is the fifth person — the fifth traveller to go with Smale to wherever they're going,' Georgie began.

'A cricket match in the past?' I suggested.

Georgie nodded, taking a drink. 'So, Smale thinks someone's coming because the fifth person has replied.'

'Only he hasn't,' I said.

'Exactly, but Smale doesn't know that. What if this guy's daughter, Jessica, went instead of him?'

'But didn't you say they're on holidays?'

'Yes, exactly,' Ally said, pointing at me.

'Riiiiight,' I said, slowly.

The two girls looked at me.

'But how does Jessica go if she's not here?' It seemed pretty straightforward to me.

'Jessica doesn't go,' Ally said quietly. 'I go.'

There was a shout from the TV. The Aussies had just taken another wicket.

'You go?' I asked. Ally nodded.

'Brilliant, huh?' said Georgie.

'Tell me how it's brilliant,' I said.

'Smale doesn't know me from Adam,' Ally explained.

'Don't be daft —'

'Wait on!' Georgie said, glaring at me. 'Let the girl finish.'

I sighed, popped the last mouthful of hamburger into my mouth and turned back to Ally.

'Smale won't recognise me,' she said. 'I'll explain that I'm Jessica, Geoff Walter's daughter, and that I'll be taking the trip on his behalf.'

'Told you it was brilliant,' Georgie repeated.

'Okay,' I sighed, grabbing another hamburger. 'First, you said yourself, Ally, that Jessica is two years older than you. Second, you say Mr Smale won't recognise you. Except he's just spent the entire afternoon watching you play a game of cricket. And third . . .'

'Third?' Ally said, smiling and looking like she didn't have a care in the world.

'Third? Um, yeah, well, third is that there's no way Smale will let a girl travel with him and a group of adults. He's probably asking them to pay ten thousand bucks each for the privilege.'

'Great. So let's just do nothing, hey?' Ally said, looking at Georgie. 'Let's sit on our backsides here, eat hamburgers and —'

'Okay!' I shouted. Nat looked up sharply. She had been talking happily to her 'friends'.

Georgie turned to her. 'Bet you haven't got Aussiebear,' she said out of the blue.

'Nope.' Nat was surprised. 'Have you?'

'It was the first one I got. You want me to get it for you?'

'Would you?' she asked, no longer troubled by my outburst.

'Cool!' Georgie raced out of the room with Nat hard on her heels.

'Okay, so how do you plan to do it?' I said, turning to Ally.

'No probs. I . . . well, *we* go down to the Scorpions' clubrooms, and I'll go in on my own and explain the situation. If I can't go on the tour, then we just go back home.'

'But what if he does recognise you?'

156

Ally shrugged. 'I guess I'll just skedaddle.'

'Yeah, and hope that Smale doesn't —'

'Toby, Smale will be occupied with the other people there. I'm going to be hanging around at first, like I just happened to be there. Then, if he does recognise me, we haven't given anything away. He'll simply tell me to run away.'

'And you will?'

'And I will.'

Georgie and Ally had the evening all planned. I headed to Georgie's house at 8.30 to 'watch a DVD'. Ally had made a similar arrangement, while Georgie was supposedly going over to Ally's. We all hopped on our bikes and rode towards the Scorpions' ground. Ally looked completely different. Her long dark hair was now bunched up on her head, and her eyes appeared darker. Maybe it was the make-up. She had neat-looking clothes on and seemed taller and older.

'You can stop staring at her,' Georgie hissed as we rode onto the street.

'I'm not!'

'Not what?' Ally called from in front.

'Totally preoccupied with the game tomorrow,' Georgie finished with a grin.

There were lights on at the Scorpious' rooms and four vehicles in the car park when we arrived.

'If he does look suspicious straight away,' Georgie said, 'just say you came back because you left your hat or something here.'

'Okay.' Ally leaned her bike up against the cemetery fence that ran behind the car park. 'Will you wait for me?'

'If you're not back in fifteen minutes, we'll assume you made it in.' Georgie looked at me.

'Which means it should be about an hour at the most before you're back,' I added.

'Hopefully not more,' Georgie grimaced.

I had a thought. 'Ally, listen! If it does look like you're going on this trip, see if you can sneak out just for a moment and tell us where you're going. That way, if there's any trouble, I —'

'We!' Georgie interrupted.

'*We* can come and help you.'

Georgie and I wheeled the bicycles behind a nearby old scout hall and sat down on the grass to wait. I guess we both expected Ally to be back pretty quickly, but after ten minutes of chatting about the grand final and what might happen tomorrow, our conversation dried up as we thought of Ally and what might be happening.

'Should we go and take a look?' I asked.

Georgie nodded. 'If they've gone there'll be no one there anyway.'

There were fewer lights on in the clubrooms now, only a glow from a room behind Smale's office. We hadn't been in there before. All the outside doors and windows appeared to be locked, except for one window that was open just a few centimetres.

We crept over to the open window, freezing when we heard a man's voice.

'Brilliant!' someone exclaimed, and there was the sound of hands clapping.

'He must be showing them something,' I whispered. 'Maybe the scorecard?' I edged away from the building.

But Georgie wasn't listening. She'd picked up a piece of paper that had been half-pushed out from beneath the main door.

'Brisbane, 19 ...' Georgie stopped reading and looked up at me.

'What?' I said, snatching the paper from her.

'Toby!'

'Brisbane, 1960. Tied Test,' I read aloud. Ally had already been there. This was a disaster. I turned to Georgie.

'I know, I know,' she groaned. 'It was a slight chance.'

'*Slight* chance?'

'Well don't you get so high and mighty,' Georgie fired back. '*You* took her there. *You* knew as well as anyone else.'

We both paused, breathing heavily, staring at each other. I couldn't remember Georgie and me ever fighting before. Not once had we had a cross word for each other.

Georgie closed her eyes and sighed. 'Toby, we're not going to get anywhere standing here arguing. What will we do?'

'The problem is we don't know if she's in any trouble. She may be fine. If there's enough distance or time between her two selves ... oh, hell!'

'What?'

'When I took her to the game — it was near the end, obviously — there was something wrong ...'

'Toby, there's always something wrong with us when we go back in time. Rahul in India. Jimbo, watching his dad. And Jay! God, remember what he did down in Hobart?'

'No, this was different. Ally was really scared. She kept looking around, and she said something about someone calling her name.'

'Smale?'

I shrugged. 'I dunno. Maybe.'

Georgie pulled a pencil from her pocket and scrawled a note on the back of the one Ally had written.

'And how will we get that to her?' I asked.

'I'll just put it on her bike. We've got to try something.'

I sat down with my back against the brick wall of the clubrooms and watched Georgie walk along the fence line to the bikes leaning against the scout hall.

'Maybe we should give it a few more minutes?' I said, looking at my watch as she returned.

'How long has it been?' Georgie asked.

'Well, we don't know how long they've been away,' I replied, 'but it's nearly half-past nine. Let's give it a few more minutes.'

While we waited, we checked out the cars parked nearby and paced around the clubrooms.

'Toby!' Georgie whispered, beckoning me over to the open window. She had pushed a section of curtain to one side, and I put my head next to hers and listened.

'They're back.' She spoke softly.

'Or they haven't gone yet. Can you see Ally?'

Holding up a hand, Georgie shook her head. There didn't seem to be the excitement in the room that we'd heard earlier.

'But what about Colin?' someone said, his voice rising above the others. A door banged shut.

'There's something wrong,' Georgie said, looking worried and backing away from the window.

'What?' I leaned in closer, trying to hear what was happening. I heard a few more shouts before Georgie grabbed at my sleeve. Something was about to happen. Crouching, we ran back to the fence, then along the side of the cemetery, to our bikes.

'We shouldn't have let her go, Toby,' Georgie said, slamming her helmet on and grabbing her bike. 'Let's go down to the end of the street and wait a few minutes.'

'I'd love to know what's happened,' I said.

'C'mon, Ally. Where *are* you?' she screamed into the wind as we tore off down the road.

'Guys!' came a shout from behind, just as the words left Georgie's lips.

We braked hard and swung our bikes around, amazed to hear Ally's voice. She was riding hard, trying to catch up with us.

Georgie dropped her bike and gave her a hug. We walked our bikes home, not only because it was dark and Ally was out of breath, but so we could hear the whole story before we got there.

In 1926, Clarrie Grimmett — playing for South Australia against New South Wales — had 394 runs scored from his bowling. This is the most runs scored off a bowler during a match in Australia, however his haul of 10 wickets (4 for 192 in the first innings and 6 for 202 in the second) is a great achievement.

18 Back to Brisbane

ONCE Ally began retelling her adventure, the words poured out like a torrent. She was still wound up by all the excitement.

'Guys, I was so nervous I thought Phillip Smale would hear my heart pounding, but I walked straight up to him and said G'day, because my disguise was pretty good and I knew I had to act like I was meant to be there.'

'And he didn't recognise you?' I asked as we picked our way carefully along the dim footpath.

'No. He just said, "Don't be ridiculous. I'm not taking any children. This isn't a game, you know."' Ally smiled. 'But one thing I didn't tell you guys, is that I'd typed up a fake letter from my "Dad", saying why he'd sent me along in his place.'

'Hey, that's a good idea,' Georgie said.

'Smale didn't want to look at it at first,' Ally continued, 'but when he read how much money my

"Dad" was offering, he decided it was okay for me to go — as long as I stayed in the background and didn't bug him.

'Then he got us all together, sitting on a big couch. There were two other men there, as well as a lady. Smale had this big screen set up, and he gave a speech, saying why we were all there. He'd asked one of the guys, Rick, along, because he was a businessman, the other guy, Colin, because he'd worked in theatre and stuff, and the lady, Davina, because she knew the media.'

'And what about Mr Walters — Jessica's dad?' I asked. 'Why had he been chosen?'

'Apparently he's a really well-known guy in banking. I didn't really know what Smale was talking about, so I just nodded and played along.

'Anyway, then he showed a bit of the Tied Test on the big screen. The others didn't know what was going on, and they were pretty annoyed that he'd got them all there just to show them an old cricket match. That's when I slipped away to leave you the note — I said I was going to the toilet but I don't think Smale heard me, because he was too busy trying to calm everyone down.

'When I got back he asked us all to hold hands while he fiddled around with a *Wisden* and an old scorecard. It must have been that magic one, Toby, because the next thing I knew we were in Brisbane in 1960.'

'What happened when you got there?' Georgie said. 'How did they all react?'

'Well, at first they didn't realise that they'd gone back in time. They thought it was some kind of virtual reality. Then as it started to sink in, the guy called Rick started to freak out — he looked really frightened and turned white. Davina stayed calm, but the other guy, Colin, was so excited, until Smale told him they wouldn't be staying to watch one of the most famous overs ever played.'

'I bet he didn't like that,' I murmured.

'Smale tried to tell us all to stay put, but Colin ignored him and ran off into the crowd because he didn't want to leave. Smale spent about twenty minutes trying to find him, but he'd disappeared.

'And that was it. The rest of us came back and I got out of there as quickly as I could ... Oh, I almost forgot! Toby, you know that Master Blaster thing you guys played down at the shopping centre?' Ally added, as we reached her front gate.

'The virtual cricket?' I said.

'Yeah, well you were right, Toby. It was there in the clubrooms. I reckon Phillip Smale has bought that too.'

'Bought, or stolen?' Georgie said, looking at me. 'And what about Alistair? Have you rung yet?'

'Yep, I finally got through, but the person who answered said he's out of town for the next few days and they're not sure when he's due back.'

'So, it's just as we thought,' Georgie said. 'Smale's going to open up a business.'

'Yeah, and it looks like he's gathering a few people around him to help out,' Ally said.

'Like that Davina woman?' Georgie asked.

'Yep.'

'But not Colin,' I muttered.

'Do you reckon Smale will go back and rescue him?' Georgie said.

'He was going to leave Scott, remember?' I answered. 'I wouldn't trust Phillip Smale.'

'I agree,' said Ally. 'We get the scorecard now and we kill this once and for all.'

Georgie and I looked at each other.

'How long have we got before Colin is in serious trouble?' I asked.

Georgie looked at her watch. 'An hour? Hour and a half, tops.'

'Okay,' I said, my mind racing. 'I'm going to get Jim and his car. You two, go home and grab your mobiles, then come back here and let me know what's happening. Stay down, but watch to see if Colin returns. Keep an eye on the cars, okay?'

'Have you got yours?' Ally asked, as I hopped onto my bike.

'My what?' I called.

'Your mobile!'

I pulled it out of my pocket and held it up behind me as I sped off.

Ten minutes later, just as I pulled up in front of Jim's, it rang.

'Anything happening?' I asked.

'Toby, all the cars have gone and the lights are all out,' Georgie said. 'We reckon he's packed up and gone.'

'He must have gone home. I'm going to head over there with Jim. We've got to nail this. Especially as that guy is stuck in Brisbane and I can't go back to get him because I've been there before.'

'That's why we need the scorecard, isn't it?' Georgie said.

'Yep. It's gonna have to be you, Georgie.'

'Okay, we'll meet you over there —'

'No! You guys stay low. I'll get back to you.'

'Hey,' Georgie cried, sounding annoyed. 'Since when —'

'Georgie. Just me and Jim, alright?' There was a pause. 'George?'

'Yeah, fine,' she mumbled.

Jim was delighted to see me and even more delighted to be getting back into Pixie, which was surprising.

'I thought you agreed it was a good idea to take a break from all this till the game was over,' I said, as we reversed out of his garage.

'Indeed I did, Toby. Indeed I did. But *carpe diem*, my boy.'

'*Carpe diem?*'

'Seize the day, Toby. Strike while the iron's hot.' Jim was raving on but he was genuinely excited. I just hoped not too excited — Jim was having adventures that most people his age wouldn't want to know about. 'At least your mind isn't stuck on the game,' he added.

That was one good spin on all this, I realised.

As we drove to Smale's place I outlined the evening's events.

'So, this Colin chap is still at large in Brisbane?' Jim said, frowning.

I nodded.

'Dear oh dear,' he murmured, accelerating a little.

'I bet I know whose car that is,' I said, pointing to one parked outside Smale's house as we drew up to the kerb.

'One of Ally's travelling partners?' Jim suggested.

I nodded.

'I think we should simply take the direct approach, Toby. Straight to the front door.'

I followed a few paces behind Jim as he marched up the path and knocked on the door.

'Who is it?' a woman's voice called, a moment later.

'Jim Oldfield.'

'Are you a friend of Phillip's?' There was no sign of the front door being opened. Maybe this was Davina. I took out my phone and dialled Ally, moving a few steps away from the house.

'Ally? What was that Davina lady wearing?' I whispered into the phone.

'Um, grey trousers and a white shirt. Why?'

'There's a lady in Smale's house and, hang on ...'

Jim was walking back towards me. 'It appears our friend Phillip is out for the evening,' he said.

'I'll call you back, Ally,' I said, snapping the phone closed. 'Now what?'

'I'm not exactly sure,' Jim replied.

We both turned at the sound of shouting.

'Let's try the back,' I urged, setting off around the side of the house. 'The door's open,' I whispered to Jim, who arrived a few moments after me. I eased it open further and then we were inside.

Jim put a finger to his lips as we snuck into the kitchen. There were voices coming from the next room — Smale's and the woman's.

'A partnership,' Smale was pleading. 'You don't know how to operate the scorecard anyway,' he continued. Their voices stopped. Jim and I stepped cautiously back, away from the door. Suddenly it burst open. Phillip Smale stood there, glaring at us.

'You interfering old man,' he growled, moving towards Jim. I stepped in front of him, reaching into my pocket at the same time. 'Get out of my way, you snivelling little boy!' He pushed me to one side. I opened the phone, carefully felt for the second number along, and pressed it. It was the autodial number for Ally's mobile.

'Davina, call the police,' Smale shouted through the kitchen door.

'Yes, do that,' Jim said. 'I'm sure they will assist Toby and me to get back what is rightfully ours.'

'What are you raving on about?' Smale said.

Jim was standing upright and perfectly at ease beside the table. 'The scorecard, of course,' he replied firmly, not taking his eyes off Smale.

My heart was racing, and, I guessed, despite his outward calm, so was Jim's.

'Jim, maybe we should just leave,' I whispered.

'Not this time, sonny,' Smale said.

'Are you a friend of Jessica's?' Davina asked, coming to the door, a phone in her hand.

'Who?'

'You heard me.'

'I don't know any Jessica,' I said, trying to sound calm.

'Just ring the bloody police,' Smale said, his anger rising.

'I'm not sure that's such a good idea,' she replied, eyeing Jim closely. 'What do you know about this scorecard?'

'Quite a bit,' Jim said. 'It was sent to me, you see —'

'Don't listen to this senile old fool,' Smale hissed, grabbing the phone from her. 'He's talking through his hat.'

'Might I sit down, please?' Jim asked, pulling out a chair.

'Of course you may.' Davina sat down too.

'Oh, for heaven's sake,' cried Phillip. 'Do you want me to do tea and biscuits?'

Jim looked up and smiled sweetly. 'What a splendid idea, Phillip. It's just like old times.'

Smale, looking furious, stormed out of the room.

'Old times?' Davina asked.

Jim explained his connection with Phillip at the MCC library and how Smale had come to know about the scorecard. Davina, who had formally introduced herself, got up and made us all a drink while Jim continued his story.

'Jim, perhaps we should go,' I said to him as he gratefully sipped the tea Davina had given him.

Suddenly the house was plunged into darkness. Jim and I reached out at the same time, grabbing hold of each other. I heard Davina shoot up like a cat and dart into the hallway.

'Phillip?' she called.

'Let's go, Jim,' I said, guiding him towards the back door.

'Toby, we need that scorecard. I feel that now is our best chance.' His voice was desperate and he seemed to be breathing heavily.

'Then I'll go. You head outside and wait in Pixie.'

'No!' he said firmly. 'Come on. This is it.'

So we crept back through the kitchen, groping for the doorway leading to the hall. Then the lights came back on. We searched the house, but there was so sign of Smale.

'Toby?' a voice called from outside. It was Georgie.

I ran to the front door and opened it to find Georgie and Ally standing there.

'Is everything okay?' Ally asked. 'We just got this garbled sort of —'

'Oh, yeah,' I said, pulling out my mobile and switching it off. 'Things hotted up in there for a moment so I opened up the line.'

We headed back inside. Davina and Jim were in a small room, obviously Smale's study, staring at a row of *Wisden*s.

'He's gone,' Jim sighed, turning as we entered.

'What the —?' Davina said, her eyes narrowing.

'Oh,' Ally said, giving her a small wave. 'Hi!'

'Jessica! So, you two *do* know each other.' She looked at me coldly.

I ignored her. 'Jim, we have another problem,' I said, turning to him.

'Oh?' He picked up a 1960 *Wisden* from the desk. But as he leafed through it, it dropped onto the desk in front of him, caught the edge and fell to the floor. I couldn't believe that Jim would drop a book, especially a cricket book — and a *Wisden* at that.

One moment he was standing there, the next he'd fallen to his knees and his face had gone deathly white.

'Toby!' Georgie gasped, rushing forward

'Jim?' I whispered, panicking, dropping down beside him.

'Stand back,' Davina said, crisply. 'Jessica, call triple zero. You,' she said, nodding at Georgie, 'run out and check the house number. Toby, get some water. Quickly!'

As we all left the room my mind was blank. I knew Jim wasn't well, but his collapse was such a shock.

Georgie was giving Ally the address for the ambulance as I returned with a glass of water.

'Leave it there,' Davina said, not turning round. 'Now off you go.'

'But I can't —'

'I said off you go. I know what I'm doing.'

'But what's happened?' I asked, as I stared at Jim lying on the floor.

'It's hard to say. Perhaps he's had a mild heart attack, or he may just have fainted. His breathing's quite steady and his pulse is rapid and fluttery but not weak. That's a good sign. But I suggest you leave now, before the cavalry arrives.'

'The cavalry?' Georgie asked from the doorway.

'I'm expecting the ambulance *and* the police,' she said. Gently she settled a cushion beneath Jim's head.

'Come on,' said Ally, glancing at her watch. 'We're way over time.'

I walked over to Jim and gave his old hand a squeeze while Davina fussed with something nearby. Suddenly I felt a firm hand grip my wrist; I looked at his face. One eye gleamed and the other winked. I felt another squeeze and then he let go as Davina turned back to him.

I hurried out of the house after Ally and Georgie, telling them that I thought Jim was just fine.

'What?' Georgie said.

'I think he was just making sure we were out of the way when the police came. Smale's onto us big time.'

'I'd rather arrive home on my own feet than in the back of a police car,' Ally said, starting to run.

When Shane Warne claimed the wicket of Marcus Trescothick in the Third Test of the 2005 Ashes series, Warne became the first bowler to take 600 Test wickets. He achieved this remarkable record in his 126th Test match.

19 So Close

Sunday — morning

SUNDAY morning was bright and sunny. I headed back to the Scorpions' ground, this time in the family car. Jim was right — the distractions of the night before had kept me from worrying about the game. I just hoped that Jim really was okay. What if the wink had just been a blink? No, it can't have been.

I felt surprisingly fresh as I stroked Mr Pasquali's practice deliveries neatly back to him.

'It's time to play the innings of your life, Toby,' he said, grinning. 'I'll be out there with you, though there's not much I can do. Good luck and enjoy it.'

Watching Scott Craven warming up was making that very hard to do, but I was determined to stay positive, play my shots and see what happened. Isn't that what the Aussie team did when it was in a corner? Those players didn't shrivel up and die; they stayed calm and confident, believing in their ability to get themselves out of strife.

And after four overs my confidence was sky high. I'd played Scott with the full face of the bat, picking off occasional singles and even a four that whistled past point and down to the fence.

'It'll come, Scotto,' the Scorpions players kept calling out.

'Not if I can help it,' I muttered under my breath. Every ball was a new challenge. I was doing it for Jim; I was doing it for Dad; I was doing it for Riverwall and my team-mates sitting on the boundary. And I was doing it for myself.

We hadn't made many runs and we'd lost Cameron and Rahul (who had been promoted in the order ahead of Jimbo), but when Mr Pasquali called for drinks, I finally looked up at the scoreboard.

Jones, 28 not out. Jimbo was on 7 and the overall score was 3 for 62.

'Job one: make them bat again,' Jimbo said, taking a drink. 'Job two: make them worry. It's you and me, Toby.'

Scott bowled two more overs after the break, but his pace had dropped. We still played him with respect, but the Scorpions sensed we were playing it safe and waiting for the next bowler. They spread the field out more, but Jimbo and I were able to knock up ones and twos with much more ease.

I looked over at Mr Pasquali at one point. He nodded, gently tapping his temple with one finger. I knew what he meant: play smart and don't get sucked in and try to score big fours and sixes.

By lunch we'd taken the score along to 3 for 131. The game had changed.

'Scott will resume after lunch,' Mr Pasquali said to Jimbo and me while munching on a chicken sandwich. 'Put that entire morning out of your head and start again. The job is *not* done, you hear?'

We both nodded.

The rest of the team left us alone — no one wanted to break the spell that had come over the game. Even Jay, usually always on for a chat, kept his distance.

Scott Craven did come back on and he bowled as fast as I'd ever seen him. Jimbo was struck on the helmet when he tried a hook shot, but he stood his ground, hardly flinching. Scott walked up close to him, but Jimbo just turned away to adjust his helmet.

The next ball was in the same spot but this time Jimbo was onto it. He smashed it magnificently over backward square leg. It crashed into a huge gum tree about halfway up the trunk then dropped onto the gravel road beneath, along with a dead branch.

The yelling and cheering from the boundary and the sense of excitement amongst the spectators was in total contrast to the mood on the field. The Scorpions were struggling, and they weren't used to that. It was the most critical time of the game.

Jimbo and I pressed on, scoring another 44 runs before I got out. It was getting too easy and I lost concentration, lazily wafting my bat at a ball pitched well outside off-stump. It caught the bottom edge and cannoned back into the stumps. I'd made 71 — my highest score ever!

Jimbo went on to make 91 but, as in the first innings, our batting performance fell away quickly. We lost our last seven wickets for only about 60 more runs. But we were in with a chance, and when Mr Pasquali told us that the whisper around the ground was that the Scorpions might be 'chasing the outright', I felt our chance of success was even greater.

We'd finished with 234 runs and the Scorpions needed 147 for an outright win.

'They don't *have* to get the runs, do they?' Martian asked, adjusting his hat. The sun was getting higher and the temperature was rising.

'Oh, no,' Mr Pasquali said. 'They just have to survive — then they win the game on the results of the first innings. But somehow I don't think they'll settle for that.'

'How many overs are left, Mr P?'

'We have to bowl 38,' he replied.

'Less if we get them all out,' I said, catching the new ball that Mr Pasquali tossed to me.

He smiled. 'Exactly.'

By the time Scott Craven marched to the crease, the game was evenly poised with the Scorpions at 4/81. They'd held Scott back, maybe hoping to get well toward the target before bringing him on. Their scoring rate was down a bit: at the start of the innings they'd needed just under four runs an over to win. Now, with 15 overs left, they needed 4.3.

We were able to pick up wickets at fairly regular intervals, but Scott was like a rock. There were no fireworks from him, just careful batting and good placement of the ball.

With two overs to go the Scorpions were 8/134, and Scott was in control. We brought the fielders in, hoping to keep their number 10 batter on strike. He didn't score off any of Rahul's first three balls, but nicked the fourth past gully for a single. Then Scott blocked Rahul's last two deliveries.

I took the ball for the last over of the match — the last over of the season. Jono and I had a long talk about the field before settling on three slips, a gully, point, cover, short mid-off, short mid-wicket and a fine leg. It was a stacked off-side field.

Scott ambled down and said a few words to his partner before returning to the non-striker's end.

I looked at the spot on the pitch I was aiming for, then strode in to the wicket.

The batter pushed across his crease, expecting a ball on or outside his off-stump even before I'd bowled. It was exactly what I was hoping he'd do, and instead I bowled a fast yorker that smacked into the bottom of his leg stump.

Scott swore, tossing his bat to the ground. They were 9/135.

We were one wicket away from winning the championship, but the Scorpions needed to survive five balls.

I pitched the next delivery right on middle stump. Their number 11 batter pushed at it, spooning the ball back towards me. I lunged desperately but it was dropping fast. I flung out my left hand, aware that as he flashed past me Scott was screaming at the other guy to run. I got a fingertip to the ball, nothing more. It trickled harmlessly down the pitch as the batters completed their run.

Had I just dropped the championship trophy?

There were just four balls left and now Scott was on strike. The Scorpions were eight runs away from an outright victory.

I brushed down my pants and told Jono that I wanted a change in the field. Maybe I should tempt Scott — what was there to lose? I beckoned to Jason, who was at fine leg, to come squarer, and moved Jimbo out of third slip to mid-wicket, about 15 metres off the boundary. Scott looked on nonchalantly, resting on his bat.

'Come on, Toby, let's have him!' Georgie yelled.

I banged the third ball in short. Scott seemed to be in two minds, but at the last moment he pulled out of a hook shot and the ball sailed through to Ally.

I did exactly the same with the next ball and this time Scott was onto it, belting it way over Jimbo's head.

The tense silence of the last few minutes was broken by a dozen car horns blaring approval.

Suddenly the Scorpions had jumped to 142. Another four would tie the game but give the Scorpions the championship because of their higher first innings total.

'Do you want to make a change?' Jono asked me from the slips.

I shook my head. What would Scott expect? Another short one? Could he afford to risk a hook shot? I watched him from the top of my run-up before checking the field, and Jimbo out at mid-wicket in particular.

'Jimbo,' I called. 'Move round five?' With my hand, I indicated that he should come closer to mid-on. This might create some doubt in the batter's mind. It was my only chance.

I ran in hard to bowl the second last ball of the game. It was short again, but wider outside the off-stump. Sure enough, Scott went for it, trying to pull it square. It caught the end of the bat and flew away towards third man. All the slips raced after it, Jono eventually hauling it in, only centimetres from the boundary.

The batters had run three which put Scott up at my end and the Scorpions on 9 for 145.

Our eyes met as I brushed past him. 'It's not over yet,' I said quietly.

'As good as,' he sneered, tearing off his gloves. He knew he'd stuffed up in going for that third run. Scott walked down and spoke to the number 11, who looked nervous and was fidgeting with his pads and helmet.

Meanwhile, Jono and I brought every fielder in closer, to try and stop them getting a single.

An eerie silence settled over the ground as I waited at the top of my mark. There were even some cars that had pulled over — maybe the drivers had noticed the larger than normal crowd for a junior cricket match, or maybe they were just curious. People out walking their dogs had stopped to look, and a bunch of kids over on the playground had crept closer during the last few overs. I noticed an old man standing just to one side of a tree way past fine leg. Somehow he looked familiar — he looked very much like Jim.

I looked down at the ball in my hand, positioned the seam upright, and charged in. As the ball left my hand I watched it sail through the air, on a perfect line outside off-stump. The batter swung at it, cross-batted and connected. I dived full-stretch to my right, knocking the ball down.

Scott had charged out of his crease, thinking the ball had gone past me. 'Run, idiot!' he yelled, before realising that I was gathering up the ball.

'No!' the other guy yelled, holding up a hand. Scott stopped dead and scrambled round desperately. Still kneeling on the ground, I backhanded the ball at the stumps. Scott dived for the line, his bat reaching out, as the ball smacked into the off-stump.

The whole Riverwall team roared in appeal.

Mr Pasquali grimaced, then slowly nodded and raised his right index finger to the sky.

 182

Scott swore and smashed his bat into the ground. There was a horrible cracking sound. For a moment the shouts, cheers and car horns all stopped; then they started up again — even louder this time.

I'd run Scott out by about half a metre. I lay back on the grass in sheer relief as my Riverwall team-mates rushed towards me.

Glenn McGrath was the last Australian to take a hat-trick in a Test match. He achieved this feat in Perth against the West Indies in 2000. In all, eight Australians have taken hat-tricks, and Thomas (Jimmy) Matthews and Hugh Trumble have each taken two. Matthews bagged his hat-tricks on the same day in 1912, but in different innings!

20 Trouble for Ally

Sunday — afternoon

MR Pasquali interrupted the post-game celebrations to announce that the awards presentation would not be taking place at the Scorpions' clubrooms. Georgie caught my eye.

'No one can find our manager,' one of their players told us.

'Mr Smale?' Ally asked.

'Yeah. He's just vanished. He hasn't been seen all day. He's the only one with the keys.'

'Toby!' Dad called, waving frantically. He was holding a mobile phone to his ear.

'It is Jim?' I shouted, racing over to him.

Dad nodded.

'Jim?' I said into the phone. 'Are you okay?'

'Hello, my boy. I'm on the mend. Peter has told me all about your exploits today.'

'I think someone's got a video of the game. Maybe we can watch it together?'

'Perhaps I'll get along to see some of the game one day,' he chuckled. The man behind the tree flashed into my mind.

'Jim! I think —'

'Listen, Toby. There's another matter you need to attend to, and without the scorecard only you can do it.'

I knew Jim was talking about the man left behind in Brisbane. 'But Smale's disappeared,' I said, moving away from Dad. 'Maybe he's gone back to get Colin?'

'Absolutely not,' Jim answered quickly. 'He has other problems to deal with.'

'What problems?' I asked. 'And anyway, we've run out of time. Remember, you've only got two hours when you go back into the past.'

'Two hours, yes, then slowly the body starts to fade. All this is true.' Jim's voice had become so soft I could barely hear him. 'But the fading process takes a while.'

'How long?'

'It varies. It depends on your age, your degree of fitness, how far away from your own time you've travelled, whether you're the carrier, or being carried ... many things.' Jim was silent a moment. 'Toby. It is time to destroy the scorecard and stop our travels. I have promised Peter that I will come and live with you. But you must promise me that after this final travel, we will both stop our journeys. We will focus on the present and the future.'

'Jim?' I said, after a pause.

185

'Yes, Toby?'

I took a deep breath. 'I agree,' I said firmly.

'Good. You'll have to take young Ally with you, but make sure you hold her hand, alright?'

'Yes, Jim —'

'And don't you let go.'

After I hung up the phone I realised that if Jim had travelled to the game, he wouldn't know about it for some time. An international one-dayer was being played in Melbourne today, but it wasn't in any *Wisden* — not yet, anyway.

Perhaps he'd simply gotten out of his sickbed and come to the game in Pixie.

Mum and Dad were determined to make up for the disappointment of the presentation night being cancelled, so they'd invited the whole team, including Mr Pasquali, back to our house for a party. On our way home we'd made a brief detour to the shops for supplies — it was going to be a big night.

Half the team had already arrived, and the rest were on their way. We were watching the last half hour of Australia's innings in the one-dayer, when the news came on the telly.

'Peter, quick!' Mum called, standing at the door. A few moments later Dad arrived in time to hear the report.

'And although police are drawing no links yet between the two, local film director and arts administrator Colin Dempsey is also missing.'

The camera showed a woman standing in front of her house, clutching two sobbing children. *'He left last night. He was only going to be away an hour,'* she explained, sounding desperate. *'Colin,'* the woman pleaded, staring into the camera, *'whatever is troubling you, please come back.'*

'Anyone with information . . . '

I didn't wait to hear any more. Ally sprang up and rushed out of the room, so I followed her out the back.

'Are you okay?' I asked.

Mum arrived a moment later. 'Ally, is everything alright, dear?'

She nodded. 'Sorry, Mrs Jones. It's j . . . just that —'

'Ally thought she recognised one of the kids,' I explained. 'We'll be back in a tick.'

Georgie slipped past Mum, who was heading back to the lounge.

'Come on,' I said. 'Let's do it.'

'Go to Brisbane?' Ally said, wiping the tears from her eyes.

I nodded.

'But Ally can't go,' Georgie said. 'And nor can you. You've been —'

'Ally has to go and so do I.' Turning, I bounded up the stairs to get the *Wisden*, the girls following. 'She's the only one who can recognise Colin, and we don't have the scorecard so I have to go. Georgie, you're going to have to cover for us. Hopefully, we won't be long.'

'But, listen,' Georgie said. 'He's already dead. It's been almost a day.'

'It won't be once we get there.' I opened the *Wisden*. 'Ally, we'll do this just like last time.' I held my hand out to her.

Georgie cursed quietly and left.

'Here,' Ally said, guiding my finger to the page.

'It's a two,' I breathed.

'Yes,' she whispered, gripping my hand tighter. It happened so quickly. It was getting faster and faster each time I travelled. We tumbled gently onto a stretch of grass. We both turned to look at the scoreboard.

'Okay, we've arrived a little bit after our last visit, but not by much. Keep your head down, and don't let go of my hand, okay?' But she wasn't listening. 'Ally!'

'Toby, oh my God! There he is!'

'Ally, no!' I yelled as she burst away from me, running towards a group of people closer to the fence. 'Ally, stop!'

Then everything went into slow motion. I heard her call Colin's name, and a guy slowly turned towards us. He looked deathly pale. I could almost see through him. He tried to stand up, but stumbled, pitching forward onto his face. No one around seemed to notice. Were they too interested in the game? Or had he already disappeared from their reality?

But I really began to panic when I noticed Ally falter. As I ran towards Colin I watched in horror as Ally started floating sideways, faster and faster.

She turned to look at me, and her face was distorted in bewilderment and pain. I didn't think I would ever forget her look of terror as this incredible force took her away.

She had flown 30 metres when suddenly, as if she'd hit some invisible wall, she collapsed.

I grabbed Colin's arm, urging him to get up. 'Please,' I cried, hauling him to his feet. 'C'mon, you're about to die!'

'W ... who are you?' he said, his voice shaky and weak.

'I'll explain later. Please!' I dragged Colin towards Ally, who was lying by a bench. 'If we get away before the last ball, everything will be okay.'

Everyone we passed was glued to the action out in the middle. The final over was unfolding, the last ball about to be delivered.

'Ally?' I said urgently, bending down and shaking her. 'Ally?'

Someone turned to look at us, but quickly looked back to the game as screams and shouts broke out around us. The action on the field had everyone's attention.

I made sure I had a hold of Colin, then took Ally's hand and recited the final lines of the poem, worrying that I hadn't been either calm or clever.

> *Respect this gift. Stay calm, stay clever,*
> *And let the years live on forever.*

We arrived back in my bedroom. It was empty. I opened the door to find Rahul, Jimbo, Jay and Georgie sitting on the stairs. They all jumped up at the sight of me.

'Rahul and Jay, quick! Get this guy home,' I said as Colin staggered to the door. 'Remember the bus in India? He's got the same problem, though way more advanced. Jimbo, you be on the look out.'

'Where's Ally?' Georgie said, pushing past me as the others snuck down the stairs.

Ally lay on the floor behind me; she hadn't moved. She was breathing evenly, but slowly. Her face was pale and she looked like she was a million miles away.

'Something's happened to her,' I said. 'I need to talk to Jim.'

'Sounds like he's just coming up,' Georgie said, racing out of the room. She came back a moment later with Jim in tow.

I closed my eyes, took a deep breath and explained what had happened. 'Jim?' I said, after pouring out the whole story. 'Say something, Jim. What is it? What's happened? Will she be okay?'

Jim stooped down beside Ally. He looked deeply concerned. 'I . . . I'm not sure,' he said.

'But she's just asleep —'

'Food's ready guys!' Mum called from the bottom of the stairs.

Georgie and I looked at each other. I felt sick to the core.

'Coming in a tick, Mrs Jones,' Georgie shouted, trying to sound cheerful, as Jimbo poked his head around the door.

'How did it go?' I asked.

'Fine. That guy was hugely relieved to be back. He knew where he was and he had his keys on him, so he decided to walk to where his car is parked. We told him that he must have blacked out or something.'

'So he was heading to the Scorpions' ground?' Georgie looked over at Jimbo.

He nodded. 'Is Ally okay?'

'Not sure,' I said. 'Jimbo, grab the others and get them downstairs for a feed. Tell Mum we've just ducked out to Georgie's, but we'll be back in ten, okay?' Maybe Ally would have recovered in that time.

'Got it,' Jimbo said and headed out.

'I'll go too, but I'll be back soon,' Jim said quietly. 'I've just checked her pulse; she's in no danger,' he added.

I wondered if that comment was more for our benefit.

Georgie and I moved Ally to the bed, then sat and talked quietly for fifteen minutes until Jim returned. We were both teary by the time he gently knocked and pushed the door open.

'They're all watching the video of the game, but you're not starring yet, Toby,' he said smiling. He walked over to the bed and sat down beside Ally, taking her hand and pressing it to his cheek.

'Jim?' Georgie croaked, looking from him to Ally.

'There is going to be one more adventure after all,' he said, slowly shaking his head. 'And I'm afraid this one will be very dangerous.' Very gently he placed Ally's hand on her stomach.

'*Another* adventure? W ... what? I stuttered, catching my breath. 'Where, Jim?'

'To Lord's, Toby. To the home of cricket. To Father Time.'

'Father Time?' Georgie's head shot up and we glanced at each other.

'Ally is not well. She will wake up soon but she will be very tired, very distant and very vague. She needs our help — and soon.'

'How soon?' I whispered, looking at her peaceful face. 'What's happening to her?'

Jim sighed. 'Come along,' he said, standing. 'You did what you had to do. Ally was the only person who could take you to that man, and you have saved his life.' He put an arm on each of our shoulders. 'Let's make her comfortable.'

Georgie gently placed a pillow under Ally's head and I covered her with my doona.

'Most appropriate,' Jim chuckled, eyeing the cricket scene on it.

All I could think of was an Aussie flag being draped over the coffin of a returning soldier.

'Come along, Toby. I promise you that there is no more to be done right now. Ally is resting. Take a break, you've both earned it.'

We walked slowly to the door.

'A part of her was lost after her first visit to Brisbane, wasn't it, Jim?' I thought of some catches she'd dropped, and times when she'd looked tired. It was so unlike Ally. 'And now more of her has gone . . .'

'What do you mean more of her?' Georgie asked. 'More of what?'

'Her spirit, Georgie. Her life. Her will to live.' Jim paused. 'Everything that is Ally: her memories, alertness, vigour, motivation and enthusiasm — her will. She is very vulnerable in this state. We must watch over her carefully.'

'But why Ally?' I asked. 'What about me? I'm not suffering like she is, and I've seen myself in the past.'

'You have, Toby, but you're stronger. After all, you have the gift. No, there's something else going on here, something out of Ally's control. But I'm sure we have got her back in time,' Jim added, trying to sound more cheeful.

Downstairs we joined the rest of the group, who were cheering every wicket of the last session. Georgie and I picked at our food, pretending to be cheerful. Rahul, Jimbo and Jay kept on giving us meaningful looks that we politely ignored. When someone asked about Ally, we simply explained that she was resting upstairs, which was accepted as others had commented that she didn't seem herself.

'She's probably caught that nasty bug that's going around,' Mum said, passing out plates of chocolate cake.

'Well, well!' Dad said suddenly, 'Speak of the devil.'

There was Ally, standing at the door to the hallway. She smiled tentatively and, after a moment of hesitation, walked over to the couch where Georgie and I were sitting.

'Room for me?' she whispered, snuggling between us.

'Always,' Georgie said with a smile, putting an arm around her.

At that moment, I think I loved Georgie almost as much as cricket.

'Jim?' Dad said, staring at the TV. 'That's not you over there skulking behind that gum tree is it? Who's got the remote? Jimbo, hit the rewind button.'

Everyone leaned forward.

'There!' Dad shouted.

Jimbo hit the pause button.

'You have some explaining to do to your grandson, Jim,' Dad laughed. Meanwhile, Mum and Nat had come in from the kitchen.

'Grandson?' Jim said, sounding puzzled.

'Well, any elderly bloke who gets off his sick bed to come and watch a boy play cricket is a grandfather in my book.'

I felt tears brimming, and Ally gently squeezed my hand. Jim's arms opened wide as I sprang up from the couch and rushed over to him, hugging him tight. I buried my face in his shoulder, only partly drowning out the cheers from all around me.

'Howzat!' Dad yelled, pointing at the TV.

I looked at the screen to see I'd just run out Scott Craven and won us the championship.

'Play it again!' I shouted.

Dad rewound then slowed the tape down, taking us through those final moments frame by frame.

'Geez, Toby, you only just hit the stumps,' Georgie laughed.

It was great seeing the action on TV — the video had some great shots of the run-out and the celebrations immediately afterwards.

'I'm sure that won't be the last time young Toby here sees himself on television performing miracles on the cricket field,' Jim said, leaning back in his chair.

'Was that the doorbell?' Mum queried, getting up and leaving the room.

'And if Toby had missed the stumps?' Mr Pasquali said, as we watched yet another replay of Scott Craven being run out.

'Scott would have made his ground and the game would have been a tie,' Jimbo said.

'Yes, and the Scorpions would have got the trophy,' Rahul added.

'Did someone mention the trophy?' Mum asked, coming back into the room. 'Look what I found!' she said, revealing a shiny object she'd been hiding behind her back.

'The trophy!' I gasped, bouncing up.

'Was anyone there?' Dad asked.

'No. Just the trophy on the doorstep and a rather flash-looking car speeding away,' Mum said, shrugging.

I glanced at Georgie as I took the trophy from Mum. We both knew who had left it there. But thankfully Phillip Smale hadn't hung around. Even though we'd finished with the Scorpions I knew that we weren't done with Smale. Not yet. But Ally's problems and Jim's talk of Lord's and a final dangerous trip made Smale seem much less important.

'How about a few photos, Dad?' I said.

As the whole team, including Mr Pasquali, gathered around me, I couldn't help but grin. I knew there'd be more time-travel adventures to come, but for now I just wanted to enjoy our win.

'Everyone say "Champions",' Dad said.

We all put our hands on the trophy. 'Champions!'

Arthur Mailey has the best innings bowling figures by any Australian in a Test match. He took 9 for 121 at the MCG in the fourth game of the 1920–21 Ashes series.

Brett Lee's Cricket Tips

Like Toby and his friends, I know that it takes more than one player to win a cricket match. Each team member plays an important part in helping their team do its best ... as well as having fun along the way!

BL

1 — OPENING BATTER

In a Test match the opening batters aim to be at the crease for the whole first day of play, and therefore they take a major role in setting the foundation for a big team score. If they do the job well, their side should only have to bat once.

It is important that opening batters establish themselves, and see out the new ball and any early movement in the wicket.

2 — FIRST-DROP BATTER

The best batter in the team is usually the 'first-drop batter'. This is the person who goes in to bat when the first wicket falls. It is a challenging position because they need to be padded up, focused and ready to go

197

as soon as their team's innings begins. If the openers get off to a good start they could be sitting in the stands for hours, or they could be walking out to face the second ball of the innings.

First-drop batters need to be able to adapt their game depending on how the match is going when they take the crease. If they are in early due to a quick wicket, they need to consolidate their team's position and take on the opener's role. However, if the openers get a big score before getting out, the first-drop batter may need to go in and score quick runs late in the day.

3 – Number six batter

A batter coming in at this stage of an innings is often faced with one of two situations, each requiring different skills. If their team has been playing well and has a lot of runs on the board, the number six's job is to attack the bowlers. This will keep the run rate ticking over and take the score as high as possible within the overs or time remaining in the game.

However, a number six batter may also come to the crease at a point when the fielding team is doing well. In this case the batter must play safely, forming partnerships with all remaining batters to ensure they see out the designated overs or time while scoring as many runs as they can.

4 – Wicket keeper

A wicket keeper should act as an energy source for their team, encouraging the fielders and bowlers throughout the match. It is also important for the keeper to be confident and skilled behind the stumps — the worst sight for any bowler is a good ball that beats both the batter and the keeper.

The keeper also helps the captain set the field, as they have the best view of the fielders and where the ball is going.

Keepers should start low and rise with the ball as it approaches. A great tip is to go through a routine before bowlers start their run-up. Set your feet and get into a low stance — this will allow you to react and move left, right, up or down in response to the ball's movement once it has reached the batter.

5 — Opening bowler

Opening bowlers are given the job of getting the fielding side off on the right foot and setting up the innings. They have to bowl the correct line and length straight away without giving the batters a loose ball and, therefore, an opportunity to play a few shots and settle in. It is important to make an opening batter play as many difficult balls as possible in the first 10 overs to force mistakes and possibly get wickets.

6 — First-change bowler

First-change bowlers work with the openers as well as spinners and even part-time bowlers. They may have to take an attacking role or just apply pressure and tie up an end. As a first-change bowler you need

to have a lot of skill to be able to adjust your game
to fit whatever your team needs.

A first-change bowler can expect to bowl a lot of
overs throughout a Test or four-day game.

7 — Spin bowler

As with all bowlers, a spinner's main aim is to take
wickets. However, spin bowlers can be called upon to
play certain roles depending on the situation and the
condition of the pitch. They may be asked to tie up
an end and put pressure on a batter, which the next
bowler can capitalise on. Or, if the pitch is providing
a lot of turn and movement, a spinner might be
aggressive and go for wickets.

It is important to keep the batter guessing as to
what delivery is coming next. It is not just about
spinning the ball; a good spin bowler will use many
variations in the flight and pitch of the ball to entice
batters to play shots or simply to put doubt in their
minds.

8 — Scorer

The role of the scorer is to keep an accurate record of
the match. This information allows the players and
spectators to determine the way the match is going, as
well as individual performances throughout the game.

9 — Slips fielder

Great slips fielders spend hours and hours practising,
and as a result they rarely drop chances.

It is important for the slips fielders, as well as the wicket keeper, to be set in a well-balanced stance before bowlers start their run-up. Also, slips fielders often stand too deep, instead of in a place where the ball will carry to them. The keeper's position is a good guide as to where the slips should stand: first slip should be half a metre behind the keeper and slightly to one side (depending on whether the batter is left-handed or right-handed); second slip should be in line with or in front of the keeper.

10 — Captain

The captain is responsible for all decisions on the field. Great captains always lead by example, and they should motivate the team as well as setting the standards for the batting, bowling and fielding.

A captain should be thinking about the game constantly, as it is important to anticipate problems in the game before they occur and make any necessary adjustments to counter them.

11 — Twelfth man

The twelfth man is an integral part of a side even though he or she is not in the starting line-up. The twelfth man motivates and supports team-mates throughout the game as well as running drinks and equipment to players on the field when needed. A twelfth man also has to be ready to take the field if necessary at all times, and therefore must always be focused on the game.

1960 Australia v West Indies Scorecard

Australia v West Indies Test Match
9–14 December 1960, Brisbane, Australia
Toss: West Indies • Decision: West Indies to bat • Result: a tie

West Indies 1st Innings

Conrad Hunte c Benaud b Davidson	24
Cammie Smith c Grout b Davidson	7
Rohan Kanhai c Grout b Davidson	15
Garry Sobers c Kline b Meckiff	132
Frank Worrell (c) c Grout b Davidson	65
Joe Solomon hit wkt b Simpson	65
Peter Lashley c Grout b Kline	19
Gerry Alexander c Davidson b Kline	60
Sonny Ramadhin c Harvey b Davidson	12
Wes Hall st Grout b Kline	50
Alf Valentine not out	0
Extras (lb 3 / w 1)	4
Total (100.6 overs, run rate 4.5 runs/over)	**453**

Australia Bowling	O	M	R	W
Alan Davidson	30	2	135	5
Ian Meckiff	18	0	129	1
Ken Mackay	3	0	15	0
Richie Benaud	24	3	93	0
Bob Simpson	8	0	25	1
Lindsay Kline	17.6	6	52	3

Australia 1st Innings

Colin McDonald c Hunte b Sobers	57
Bob Simpson b Ramadhin	92
Neil Harvey b Valentine	15
Norm O'Neill c Valentine b Hall	181
Les Favell run out	45
Ken Mackay b Sobers	35
Alan Davidson c Alexander b Hall	44
Richie Benaud (c) lbw Hall	10
Wally Grout lbw Hall	4
Ian Meckiff run out	4
Lindsay Kline not out	3
Extras (b 2 / lb 8 / w 1 / nb 4)	15
Total (130.3 overs, run rate 3.9 runs/over)	**505**

West Indies Bowling

	O	M	R	W
Wes Hall	29.3	1	140	4
Frank Worrell	30	0	93	0
Garry Sobers	32	0	115	2
Alf Valentine	24	6	82	1
Sonny Ramadhin	15	1	60	1

West Indies 2nd Innings

Conrad Hunte c Simpson b Mackay	39
Cammie Smith c O'Neill b Davidson	6
Rohan Kanhai c Grout b Davidson	54
Garry Sobers b Davidson	14
Frank Worrell (c) c Grout b Davidson	65
Joe Solomon lbw b Simpson	47
Peter Lashley b Davidson	0
Gerry Alexander b Benaud	5
Sonny Ramadhin c Harvey b Simpson	6
Wes Hall b Davidson	18
Alf Valentine not out	7
Extras (b 14 / lb 7 / w 2)	23
Total (92.6 overs, run rate 3.1 runs/over)	**284**

Australia Bowling	O	M	R	W
Alan Davidson	24.6	4	87	6
Ian Meckiff	4	1	19	0
Ken Mackay	21	7	52	1
Richie Benaud	31	6	69	1
Bob Simpson	7	2	18	2
Lindsay Kline	4	0	14	0
Norm O'Neill	1	0	2	0

Australia 2nd Innings

Colin McDonald b Worrell	16
Bob Simpson c sub (Lance Gibbs) b Hall	0
Neil Harvey c Sobers b Hall	5
Norm O'Neill c Alexander b Hall	26
Les Favell c Solomon b Hall	7
Ken Mackay b Ramadhin	28
Alan Davidson run out	80
Richie Benaud (c) c Alexander b Hall	52
Wally Grout run out	2
Ian Meckiff run out	2
Lindsay Kline not out	0
Extras (b 2 / lb 9 / nb 3)	14
Total (68.7 overs, run rate 3.4 runs/over)	**232**

West Indies Bowling	O	M	R	W
Wes Hall	17.7	3	63	5
Frank Worrell	16	3	41	1
Garry Sobers	8	0	30	0
Alf Valentine	10	4	27	0
Sonny Ramadhin	17	3	57	1

1930 England v Australia Scorecard

England v Australia Test Match

11–15 July 1930, Headingley, Leeds, England

Toss: Australia • Decision: Australia to bat • Result: Match drawn

Australia 1st Innings

Bill Woodfull (c) b Hammond	50
Archie Jackson c Larwood b Tate	1
Don Bradman c Duckworth b Tate	334
Alan Kippax c Chapman b Tate	77
Stan McCabe b Larwood	30
Vic Richardson c Larwood b Tate	1
Ted a'Beckett c Chapman b Geary	29
Bert Oldfield c Hobbs b Tate	2
Clarrie Grimmett c Duckworth b Tyldesley	24
Tim Wall b Tyldesley	3
Percy Hornibrook not out	1
Extras (b 5 / lb 8 / w 1)	14
Total (168 overs, run rate 3.37 runs/over)	**566**

England Bowling	O	M	R	W
Harold Larwood	33	3	139	1
Maurice Tate	39	9	124	5
George Geary	35	10	95	1
Dick Tyldesley	33	5	104	2
Wally Hammond	17	3	46	1
Maurice Leyland	11	0	44	0

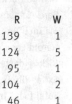

England 1st Innings

Jack Hobbs c a'Beckett b Grimmett	29
Herbert Sutcliffe c Hornibrook b Grimmett	32
Wally Hammond c Oldfield b McCabe	113
Kumar Duleepsinhji b Hornibrook	35
Maurice Leyland c Kippax b Wall	44
George Geary run out (Wall)	0
George Duckworth c Oldfield b a'Beckett	33
Percy Chapman (c) b Grimmett	45
Maurice Tate c Jackson b Grimmett	22
Harold Larwood not out	10
Dick Tyldesley c Hornibrook b Grimmett	6
Extras (b 3 / lb 10 / nb 3)	22
Total (175.2 overs, run rate 2.23 runs/overs)	**391**

Australia Bowling	O	M	R	W
Tim Wall	40	12	70	1
Ted a'Beckett	28	8	47	1
Clarrie Grimmett	56.2	16	135	5
Percy Hornibrook	41	7	94	1
Stan McCabe	10	4	23	1

England 2nd Innings (following on)

Jack Hobbs run out (Bradman)	13
Herbert Sutcliffe not out	28
Wally Hammond c Oldfield b Grimmett	35
Kumar Duleepsinhji c Grimmett b Hornibrook	10
Maurice Leyland not out	1
George Geary (dnb)	
George Duckworth (dnb)	
Percy Chapman (c) (dnb)	
Maurice Tate (dnb)	
Harold Larwood (dnb)	
Dick Tyldesley (dnb)	
Extras (lb 8)	8
Total (51.5 overs, run rate 1.84 runs/over)	**3 / 95**

Australia Bowling	O	M	R	W
Tim Wall	10	3	20	0
Ted a'Beckett	11	4	19	0
Clarrie Grimmett	17	3	33	1
Percy Hornibrook	11.5	5	14	1
Stan McCabe	2	1	1	0

Under-13 Southwestern Division

Competition Rules and Draw

There will be six teams competing for the Under-13 Cricket Cup this year.

- Benchley Park
- Motherwell State
- Riverwall Cricket Club
- The Scorpions
- St Mary's
- TCC

Competition Rules

Points

Five points shall be awarded to the winning team.

A batting point shall be awarded for every 30 runs scored.

A bowling point shall be awarded for every two wickets taken.

One-day games

The side batting second shall face the same number of overs as the side bowling first manages to bowl in 90 minutes.

Batters shall retire on making 30 runs.

Retired batters may return to the crease only if all other batters have been dismissed.

Any bowler cannot bowl more than four overs.

Two-day games

The side batting second shall face the same number of overs as the side bowling first manages to bowl in three and a half hours.

Batters shall retire on making 40 runs.

Retired batters may return to the crease only if all other batters have been dismissed.

Any bowler cannot bowl more than eight overs.

Finals

After the five round robin games have been played the following finals will be scheduled.

Semi-finals (venue — home grounds of first-named teams)

Game A Team 1 v Team 4 Game B Team 2 v Team 3

Grand final (venue — highest placed winner from semi-finals)

Winner of Game A v Winner of Game B

In the grand final there is no limit to the number of overs a bowler may bowl nor to the number of runs a batter may score. If the game is not completed, the team with the higher first innings score will be declared the winner. In the event of a draw, the team placed higher in the division will win the championship.

Draw

Round 1 (one-dayer)

St Mary's v TCC
Riverwall v Motherwell State
The Scorpions v Benchley Park

Round 2 (two-dayer)

Riverwall v St Mary's
Motherwell State v Benchley Park
TCC v The Scorpions

Round 3 (two-dayer)

Motherwell State v St Mary's
The Scorpions v Riverwall
Benchley Park v TCC

Round 4 (one-dayer)

Riverwall v Benchley Park
The Scorpions v St Mary's
TCC v Motherwell State

Round 5 (two-dayer)

Motherwell State v The Scorpions
TCC v Riverwall
Benchley Park v St Mary's

Semi-finals (two-dayer)

1st v 4th 3rd v 2nd

Grand final (two-dayer)

The winners of the semi-finals

Scores and Ladders

Points

Win 5 points
30 runs 1 point
2 wickets 1 point

ROUND 1

TCC 4/135 defeated St Mary's 5/112
Riverwall 7/164 defeated Motherwell State 107
The Scorpions 5/186 defeated Benchley Park 35 and 68

Ladder	P	W	L	Bat P	Bowl P	Win P	Total
The Scorpions	1	1	0	6	10	5	21
Riverwall	1	1	0	5	5	5	15
TCC	1	1	0	4	2	5	11
Motherwell State	1	0	1	3	3	0	6
Benchley Park	1	0	1	3	2	0	5
St Mary's	1	0	1	3	2	0	5

ROUND 2

Riverwall 8/271 defeated St Mary's 160
Motherwell State 8/214 defeated Benchley Park 6/204
The Scorpions 7/283 defeated TCC 147

Ladder	P	W	L	Bat P	Bowl P	Win P	Total
The Scorpions	2	2	0	15	15	10	40
Riverwall	2	2	0	14	10	10	34
Motherwell State	2	1	1	10	6	5	21
TCC	2	1	1	8	5	5	18
Benchley Park	2	0	2	9	6	0	15
St Mary's	2	0	2	8	6	0	14

ROUND 3

The Scorpions 9/175 defeated Riverwall 9/174
St Mary's 8/142 defeated Motherwell State 131
Benchley Park 109 defeated TCC 9/96

Ladder	P	W	L	Bat P	Bowl P	Win P	Total
The Scorpions	3	3	0	20	19	15	54
Riverwall	3	2	1	19	14	10	43
Motherwell State	3	1	2	14	10	5	29
St Mary's	3	1	2	12	11	5	28
Benchley Park	3	1	2	12	10	5	27
TCC	3	1	2	11	10	5	26

ROUND 4

Riverwall 6/191 defeated Benchley Park 170
The Scorpions 5/213 defeated St Mary's 7/106
Motherwell State 4/161 defeated TCC 118

Ladder	P	W	L	Bat P	Bowl P	Win P	Total
The Scorpions	4	4	0	27	22	20	69
Riverwall	4	3	1	25	19	15	59
Motherwell State	4	2	2	19	15	10	44
Benchley Park	4	1	3	17	13	5	35
St Mary's	4	1	3	15	13	5	33
TCC	4	1	3	14	12	5	31

ROUND 5

The Scorpions 5/282 defeated Motherwell State 9/123
Riverwall 9/256 defeated TCC 172
Benchley Park 5/198 defeated St Mary's 86

Ladder	P	W	L	Bat P	Bowl P	Win P	Total
The Scorpions	5	5	0	36	26	25	87
Riverwall	5	4	1	33	24	20	77
Benchley Park	5	2	3	23	18	10	51
Motherwell State	5	2	3	23	17	10	50
TCC	5	1	4	19	16	5	40
St Mary's	5	1	4	17	15	5	37

The Finals Series — Semi-finals

Riverwall v Benchley Park
Riverwall's home ground
Toss: Riverwall • Decision: Riverwall to bat • Result: Riverwall won by
68 runs

Riverwall Innings

Jono c Taylor b Gruff	20
Cameron retired	42
Rahul retired	41
Jimbo not out	60
Toby c Kovocev b Russell	28
Martian b Kovocev	11
Ally lbw Gruff	2
Jay run out	0
Georgie c Foley b Kovocev	3
Gavin c Rankin B Ulrich	11
Jason not out	2
Extras (b 3 / lb 3 / w 4 / nb 1)	11
Total (38 overs)	**7/231**

Benchley Park Innings   **8/163**

Riverwall Bowling	O	M	R	W
Toby	11	2	37	4
Rahul	8	1	28	2
Cameron	7	0	31	1
Jono	7	0	31	1
Jason	3	0	9	0
Jay	2	0	13	0

The Scorpions v Motherwell State

The Scorpions 5/161 defeated Motherwell State 53 and 92

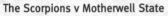

The Final Series — Grand Final

The Scorpions v Riverwall
The Scorpions' home ground
Toss: The Scorpions • Decision: Riverwall to bat • Riverwall win the
Under-13 Southwestern Division by 1 run

Riverwall 1st Innings

Jono c Taylor b Wyatt	20
Cameron c Craven b Wyatt	3
Jimbo c Blake b Wyatt	4
Rahul b Craven	0
Toby b Craven	21
Martian c Russell b Craven	6
Georgie lbw Mason	0
Minh b Craven	8
Ally lbw Mason	5
Gavin c Craven b Mason	10
Jason not out	4
Extras (b 3 / lb 2 / w 2 / nb 6)	13
Total (25 overs)	**94**

The Scorpions 1st Innings   182

Riverwall Bowling	O	M	R	W
Toby	13.5	4	35	5
Rahul	11	3	45	1
Cameron	7	0	36	1
Jono	6	0	25	1
Jason	4	0	23	0
Georgie	1	0	12	1

Riverwall 2nd Innings

Jono lbw Craven	5
Cameron c Craven b Wyatt	15
Toby b Mason	71
Jimbo c Krsul b Craven	91
Rahul b Wyatt	16

214

Riverwall 2nd Innings (cont'd)

Martian b Craven	1
Georgie b Mason	0
Minh b Craven	4
Ally not out	10
Gavin c Craven b Mason	0
Jason b Craven	0
Extras (b 1 / lb 8 / w 6 / nb 6)	21
Total (42 overs)	**234**

The Scorpions 2nd Innings	**145**

Riverwall Bowling	O	M	R	W
Toby	17	2	40	6
Rahul	9	2	43	1
Cameron	5	1	25	0
Jono	5	0	19	2
Jason	2	0	9	0

Riverwall Scores and Statistics

BATTING SCORES

Game	1	2	3	4	5
Toby	25 ret	32 ret	29	23	31 no
Scott	31 ret	6	8	35 ret	134 no
Jimbo	dnp	dnp	dnp	30 ret	18
Jono	33	57 no	0	18	11
Cameron	17	27	33 ret	15	4
Rahul	5	61 no	0	11	21
Gavin	0	19	19	12	dnp
Georgie	12	14	20	8	9
Jay	17 ret	13	13	4 no	8
Ally	dnp	1	19 no	11 no	2
Minh	0	18	dnp	1	7
Jason	dnp	dnp	20	dnp	dnp
Martian	7 no	dnp	dnp	dnp	0
Ahmazru	11	3	0	dnp	dnp
(extras)	8	20	13	23	13
Totals	**7/164**	**8/271**	**9/174**	**6/191**	**9/256**

216

BATTING SCORES (cont'd)

Game	S/F	G/F 1st Inn	2nd Inn	Total
Toby	28	21	71	260
Scott	dnp	dnp	dnp	214
Jimbo	60	4	91	203
Jono	20	20	5	164
Cameron	42 ret	3	15	156
Rahul	41 ret	0	16	155
Gavin	11	10	0	71
Georgie	3	0	0	66
Jay	0	dnb	dnb	55
Ally	2	5	10 no	50
Minh	dnp	8	4	38
Jason	2 no	4 no	0	26
Martian	11	6	1	25
Ahmazru	dnp	dnp	dnp	14
(extras)	11	13	21	
Totals	**7/231**	**94**	**234**	

BATTING AVERAGES

	Games	Innings	Not Outs	Runs	Highest	Average
Scott	5	5	3	214	134 no	107.00
Toby	7	8	3	260	71	52.00
Jimbo	4	5	1	203	91	50.75
Cameron	7	8	2	156	42 ret	26.00
Rahul	7	8	2	155	61 no	25.83
Jono	7	8	1	164	57 no	23.43
Jay	6	6	2	55	17 ret	13.75
Jason	3	4	2	26	20	13.00
Ally	6	7	3	50	19 no	12.50
Gavin	6	7	0	71	19	10.14
Martian	4	4	1	25	11	8.33
Georgie	7	8	0	66	20	8.25
Minh	5	6	0	38	18	6.33
Ahmazru	3	3	0	14	11	4.67

How to Play
Double-wicket Cricket

This game is ideally played with six pairs, and teams should be as even as possible (try to match a batter with a bowler). Each pair may be given a number or they may like to name themselves after a country or famous partnership, for example 'The Waugh twins'.

Double-wicket cricket follows the normal rules of cricket, yet there are some differences:

• Each batting pair faces six overs. These overs should be bowled by six different players.
• If a batter gets out, he or she doesn't retire, however the batting pair does switch ends.
• Each bowler bowls two overs.
• Fielders should rotate positions so that everyone has an opportunity to field in different parts of the ground.

POINTS

Wicket (bowler): 10 points
Wicket (batter): -15 points
Run-out (fielder): 5 points
Catch (fielder): 5 points
Run (batter): 1 point per run

Mr Pasquali also uses bonus points to reward good bowling and fielding. Your coach might like to do the same!

Mr Pasquali modifies these rules each year, depending on the number of cricketers available to play, and your club or team may choose to do so as well. Also, you might use a different point system — in the Double-wicket World Championship batters only lose 10 points if they are dismissed. Another feature of these championships is that a permanent team of fielders is used for all the games. This means that pairs can play each other directly; for example, Pair A bowls to Pair B, then Pair B bowls to Pair A.

You might like to visit the website of the Double-wicket World Championship to see the official rules:
www.doublewicketworldchampionship.com

For more information on double-wicket competitions and to nominate your all time favourite partner for a double-wicket competition, visit www.michaelpanckridge.com.au and follow the Toby Jones links to the double-wicket cricket page.

Results of Riverwall's Double-wicket Competition

	Batting	Wickets (Batting)	Wickets (Bowling)	Catches	Run-outs	Bonus	TOTAL
Pair 1							
Jono	22	0	20	10	0	6	58
Jason	9	-30	0	5	0	4	-12
							46
Pair 2							
Rahul	19	0	20	5	5	8	57
Gavin	13	-30	10	0	0	2	-5
							52
Pair 3							
Ally	8	0	0	0	0	4	12
Toby	25	0	30	0	0	8	63
							75
Pair 4							
Jimbo	38	0	10	10	0	10	68
Jay	6	-30	0	5	0	5	-14
							54
Pair 5							
Minh	13	-15	0	5	0	6	9
Cameron	24	0	0	5	0	6	35
							44
Pair 6							
Ivan	15	-15	0	10	0	5	15
Georgie	17	-15	10	5	0	8	25
							40

First place: Ally and Toby
Second place: Jimbo and Jay
Third place: Rahul and Gavin

MICHAEL PANCKRIDGE has worked as a teacher for more than 15 years. He has been a lifelong fan of all sports, especially cricket. Michael has both played and coached cricket but, having lost the cricket ball that the family pet Oscar recently buried, has decided to concentrate on his batting — if only he can find his bat!

Visit Michael's website at
www.michaelpanckridge.com.au

BRETT LEE grew up in Wollongong, New South Wales, and is the younger brother of former international cricketing all-rounder Shane Lee. Brett made his first-class cricketing debut in 1995 and his Australian debut against India in 1999/2000. He is one of the country's fastest ever bowlers, regularly clocking speeds of over 150 kilometres per hour.

Toby Jones and the
Magic Cricket Almanack

MICHAEL PANCKRIDGE

WITH BRETT LEE

Toby Jones and his friends are obsessed with cricket. They all play in the Under-13 school team and hang out in their own online cricket chatroom after school. Luckily, they also have a sports-mad teacher who lets them do projects on cricket.

While on a school excursion Toby visits the Melbourne Cricket Club Library, where he meets fellow cricket buff Jim Oldfield and stumbles upon the secret of the Magic Cricket Almanack. This secret, which Jim shares, is so extraordinary it could change Toby's life forever.

Life for Toby and his friends becomes a balancing act — following their passion of playing cricket while keeping Toby's new-found secret. But are they ready for the dangers this secret holds?

Toby Jones and the Magic Cricket Almanack is the first book in an exciting new series that combines cricket with fantasy. Featuring cricket commentary co-written with Australian fast bowler Brett Lee, this is a book guaranteed to leave you wanting more.

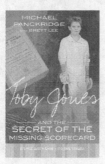

Toby Jones and the
Secret of the Missing Scorecard

MICHAEL PANCKRIDGE

WITH BRETT LEE

Toby Jones lives and breathes cricket. He plays in a local cricket competition, follows the professional players and knows all the stats. But Toby has a secret — he can travel back through time to watch famous cricket matches and players. And he can take his friends with him. But it's not all good news ...

There are dangers. Toby has seen the strange, hooded figure lurking in the background. What, or who, is this creepy character after? And how desperate is he to get what he wants?

If you love fantasy or sport, you'll love reading the Toby Jones books.

'Kids, cricket, fun — always the perfect
combination.' BRETT LEE